Savannah

Haunts of the Hostess
Tales that Still Spook Savannah

David Harland Rousseau
Illustrated by Julie Collins Rousseau

Schiffer Publishing Ltd
4880 Lower Valley Road, Atglen, PA 19310 USA

Dedication

For Hilton....

Other Schiffer Books by David Harland Rousseau
Savannah Tavern Tales and Pubs Review

Other Schiffer Books on Related Subjects
Savannah Spectres, Margaret Wayt Debolt
Ghosts! Washington Revisited, John Alexander
The Ghosts of New Orleans, Dr. Larry Montz & Daena Smoller
Ghosts of New York City, Therese Lanigan-Schmidt
Baltimore's Harbor Haunts, Melissa Rowell & Amy Lynwander

Disclaimer

The reader may notice that the names of certain streets or squares in these stories can't be found on any modern map of Savannah. Times change. Where needed, for proper historical context, the original street or square names were used instead of the contemporary names.

The reader may also notice that certain stories called for a period dialect or accent, if you will. Various pejoratives were in common usage, which are no longer acceptable. This may offend the sensibilities of certain readers. The author can only encourage such persons to go to the original sources and take careful note of the way our forebears spoke, and expressed their thoughts of their fellow man. The reader can be assured that steps were taken to respectfully preserve the "voice" of the speakers in order to place them in their proper context.

In the interest of good story telling, corners were rounded, timelines compressed, and minor characters and events were blended together. In some cases, where the original tellers of the tales are still living, names have been changed to protect their right to privacy.

Copyright © 2006 by David Harland Rousseau
Library of Congress Control Number: 2006924183

All rights reserved. No part of this work may be reproduced or used in any form or by any means— graphic, electronic, or mechanical, including photocopying or information storage and retrieval systems— without written permission from the publisher.

The scanning, uploading and distribution of this book or any part thereof via the Internet or via any other means without the permission of the publisher is illegal and punishable by law. Please purchase only authorized editions and do not participate in or encourage the electronic piracy of copyrighted materials.

"Schiffer," "Schiffer Publishing Ltd. & Design," and the "Design of pen and ink well" are registered trademarks of Schiffer Publishing Ltd.

Designed by John P. Cheek
Type set in Benguiat Bk BT/Dutch 809 BT

ISBN: 0-7643-2494-2
Printed in China

Published by Schiffer Publishing Ltd.
4880 Lower Valley Road
Atglen, PA 19310
Phone: (610) 593-1777; Fax: (610) 593-2002
E-mail: Info@schifferbooks.com

For the largest selection of fine reference books on this and related subjects, please visit our web site at **www.schifferbooks.com**
We are always looking for people to write books on new and related subjects. If you have an idea for a book please contact us at the above address.

This book may be purchased from the publisher.
Include $3.95 for shipping.
Please try your bookstore first.
You may write for a free catalog.

In Europe, Schiffer books are distributed by
Bushwood Books
6 Marksbury Ave.
Kew Gardens
Surrey TW9 4JF England
Phone: 44 (0) 20 8392-8585;
Fax: 44 (0) 20 8392-9876
E-mail: info@bushwoodbooks.co.uk
Website: www.bushwoodbooks.co.uk
Free postage in the U.K., Europe; air mail at cost.

Contents

Preface 6

Acknowledgments 9

Foreword by Robert Hunnicutt, Founder,
    Georgia Ghost Society 10

Alice Riley 14

René 32

Dreadful Pestilence 60

A Fashionable Murder 76

A Shipbuilder and his Lady 96

Come to Scratch 108

Gracie 138

Bo-Cat 154

Hag Ridden 166

No Mo' Mojo 176

Bibliography 186

Preface

All stories are true.

I'd like to amend that ancient Ibo proverb just a little, to read: "All stories are true — *especially ghost stories*."

I know. I can hear the groaning from the skeptics among you. Groan away. I didn't say, "factual." I said, "true."

You see, truth isn't judged by the same standards as are facts. Facts are things we *know*. They can be itemized, categorized, and catalogued. Truth is something we *feel*. It's greater than the sum of its parts. It's visceral.

Aren't all fables true? All myths? All legends? All parables? Of course they are.

It's a *fact* that grasshoppers and ants cannot actually speak to one another in perfect English, yet this fable is one of the first stories that we tell our children because it provides a lesson on the virtue of hard work and the vice of sloth. Since no parent wants to set a poor example to their child by lying, these stories must be true.

Still don't believe me?

A girl in a red hood encounters a talking wolf.... An ugly duckling grows into a beautiful swan.... A train (not the engineer) believes he can scale a mountain.

Something uniquely American?

A man wearing a pot for a hat wanders the countryside planting apple trees.... A rail worker bets that he can dig a tunnel faster than a machine, but dies at the finish line.... A giant lumberjack roams the land with a big blue ox as a companion.

Something in black, perhaps?

A schoolteacher in a sleepy New England town flees a headless rider.... Children lost in the woods encounter a cannibal, but manage to escape by pushing her into an oven.... A long dead cat betrays a murderer.

You get the idea.

Some of my colleagues have published interesting books that share similar stories of Savannah's ghosts, but the tales told in such books are presented to the reader as testimonials and factual events, mostly based on "eyewitness accounts" of "things that go bump in the night." With one or two exceptions (such as *Savannah Spectres*, by Margaret Wayt DeBolt), these books provide only a parenthetical historic context, and the stories themselves often lacked narrative structure. Readers found it difficult to relate to the characters, no matter how real, and wanted something more. More importantly, they wanted to be entertained.

Savannah Ghosts blends history with mystery, reintroducing the folktale — with perspective and context — to those who are hungry for a good, old-fashioned ghost story. These ten tales represent a collective unconscious of Savannah. They have been passed from family to family, from one generation down to the next, and from Savannah native to inquisitive traveler. They're stories that "Mama an' them" swear by — and all are worth retelling.

David Harland Rousseau
Savannah, Georgia, 2005

Acknowledgments

The author would first like to thank M. Hilton Swing, president and founder of The Savannah Walks, Inc., who, as mentor, took the author under his wing, and has always been a good friend.

The author would like to thank Mrs. Margaret Wayt DeBolt, historian, author, and grand matron of Savannah's ghost stories, whose book, *Savannah Spectres*, has inspired hundreds of ghost tour guides for more than two decades.

The author would also like to thank Savannah's tour guides, who keep the spirit alive (no pun intended) by telling and retelling the tales to new audiences nightly.

The author and illustrator would like to thank Robert Hunnicutt, founder of the Georgia Ghost Society, for his earnest and honest efforts to investigate and document Georgia's haunted history.

Finally, the illustrator would like to thank Jan Blackshire, who first shared the haunting tales that instilled a love for Savannah's rich history.

Foreword

The State of Georgia has been widely recognized for many influential things over the past few years, with contributions to music, athletics, and natural resources. Lately there is a topic of discussion and fascination that is now rapidly gaining notoriety, but to some has been a major source of interest for years: Georgia's ghosts and hauntings.

For almost fifteen years, I have investigated and documented ghostly activity around the Southeastern United States, focusing primarily on the vast paranormal and supernatural history of Georgia. It was obvious to me that other portions of the country, especially New England, seemed to have a monopoly of sorts on the most popular cases of paranormal activity and supernatural hauntings. The Georgia Ghost Society was created for a dual purpose: to offer assistance to those experiencing haunting phenomena in their homes and businesses, and to help publicize and promote Georgia's haunted historical locations.

In March of 2005, I received a phone call from a Boston Globe reporter who needed assistance with an article she was writing: "Savannah: The Most Haunted City in America." Her plan was to visit during the St. Patrick's Day Festival and be taken on a tour of the more haunted locations, and to gather historical background information. Because the city is extremely crowed during the festival, I decided to contact one of the city's tour companies to see if they could assist me with this project. Of all of the tours available, The Savannah Walks Ghost Tour was the most professional, dedicated to promoting both the supernatural *and* historical aspects of each location. The general manager, David Rousseau, impressed me so much from the start because he went out of his way to ensure that both the reporter and my team were taken care of. In fact, I was so impressed with both David and his staff that they are the **only** ghost tour officially recommended by The Georgia Ghost Society.

Savannah Ghosts is a great collection of Georgia's ghost stories. Far more than just spooky tales for around the campfire, these stories open a window into Georgia's past and the people who experienced them. Regardless of your age or background, you will find yourself reading these unique stories over and over again (as I have).

I am deeply honored to write the foreword to a fabulous collection of ghost stories; to make a small contribution to David's work of ensuring that this special collection of ghost lore and unique storytelling will be available for my children's children and that Georgia will be recognized for its haunted history for years to come.

Robert M. Hunnicutt
Paranormal Investigator
Founder-Director of The Georgia Ghost Society

Alice Riley

England will grow rich by sending her poor abroad.

Gen. James Edward Oglethorpe

January 1734

Alice gathered her skirts and rolled over. She'd had enough of the relentless rocking. Over the roughhewn rail she dangled her legs, her toes seeking purchase on the bunk frame below. The man below never noticed.

Lord, Richard, she thought. The man could sleep through anything.

I ought to give you a swift kick, just to see if you're alive.

Her bare feet hit the damp floor. She could feel the water leech through the floorboards. Alice crouched and blew gently into Richard's ear. He waved a hand as if he were shooing away the flies. She shook her head. For her, their relationship was one of convenience, though Richard certainly proved he was true to his word: he was, indeed, following her to the ends of the earth.

Alice stood and looked around. Some forty of her countrymen were crammed into the hold of the coffin ship, all bound for some backwater town called *Savannah*. There was barely enough room to lie in the wooden bunks, never mind milling about.

Thunder rolled overhead. Over the steady roar of the ocean, she could hear the pummeling rain.

"How long will the rains last?" she muttered. The gale had kept them below deck for days, and no one could remember the last time they had even nibbled on a scrap of hard tack.

Alice tied back her raven hair and hoisted her skirts. She padded across the narrow orlop, occasionally catching her balance with a hand on the deck beam. Just as she was about to step over a stout man slumbering, the ship lurched. Alice slipped and found herself straddling the portly gent. He awoke with a lecherous smile.

"Who has the energy?" said Alice, rolling her eyes. She patted his chest and rose to her feet. The big man rolled over and watched her saunter over snoozers, completely unaware that his watch had just been lifted.

Alice ducked through the hatch and moved to the galley in the center of the ship. The ship swayed, and Alice stumbled straight into the arms of a sailor.

"What do we 'ave 'ere?" he said, gripping her arms tightly. The ship pitched, and Alice threw herself at the swabbie.

"You weren't tryin' to sneak into the galley now, were ya?"

The ship pitched again. Alice was thrown against the bulkhead. The swabbie leaned hard against Alice.

"I'm just hungry," she said. "Surely there is something in the hold."

"We're all hungry," said the sailor. "What are you willing to do about it?"

To the delight of the seaman, Alice untied the bodice of her dress. Through a curtain of tousled hair, she smiled. The sailor ran a filthy hand across an unshaven face, unable to take his eyes off her. Gracefully, Alice dipped her delicate fingers into her cleavage, only to retrieve the chain of the gold watch she lifted from the fat man.

"Interested?" she said, dangling the watch before him. The sailor smiled and reached for the watch. Alice snatched it back, but not before the sailor seized her wrist.

"Come now, love," purred the sailor. He leaned in to whisper in her ear. "You'll never get anywhere like that."

The swabbie grinned, showing a mouthful of jagged, yellowed teeth. Alice pursed her lips, and then held up the watch. The sailor quickly plucked it out of her hands.

"Now, go on!" he said, polishing the faceplate with a grimy thumb.

"What about the food?" Alice snarled.

The sailor put his scruffy face against hers.

"Did you really think I would give up *my own* rations for a pocket watch?" He tossed the watch into the air, snatched it, and then wedged it in his waistband. He turned and started down the passageway.

"Come back tomorrow with something a little... *sweeter* and I'll think about it. If you're real good, I'll give you back the watch."

Alice shrieked. She lunged for the swabbie. She seized him by the hair and tried to drive his face into the bulkhead. The sailor wheeled around. He caught her under the shoulder and threw her to the planks. Just as he was stalking toward her, the deck hatch blew open. A hard rain poured in. Alice pressed herself against the timbers. She watched as another sailor stuck his head through the hatch.

"Forget your oilskins!" barked the sailor. "We need you on the rudder!"

Alice watched the swabbie scamper through the hole.

The hatch slammed shut. She heard the metallic grind of the latch. Alice hugged her knees and rocked herself to sleep, hunger gnawing at her belly.

Tybee Island, later that morning....

Wind snapped at his greatcoat. General Oglethorpe stomped through the mud to inspect the site's new beacon. The foundation for the ninety-foot cedar tower that would quite literally put Tybee Island and the City of Savannah on mariner's maps was nearly laid.

So much had happened in the last few months. Savannah, originally a business venture for England and the Grand Experiment, which promised to relieve the Kingdom of it's tired and poor, was quickly evolving into Georgia's First City. Nearly forty houses dotted the bluff overlooking the river for which the city was named, and the community could now boast of public ovens and wells, community squares, a courthouse (which also served as a house of worship), and, on the southwest trust lot, adjacent to the public ovens, a home for the indigent was being constructed.

These are exciting times, thought Oglethorpe.

A rain soaked messenger ran up to the General and saluted.

"General Oglethorpe!" Oglethorpe turned to the straight-as-an-arrow recruit and returned the formal salute with a very casual one.

"As you were," replied the General. "What news have you?"

"A sloop has docked near the bluff, sir."

"I watched her sail past," said Oglethorpe. He looked out over the endless Atlantic. Dark clouds blanketed the horizon. "Blown in from the storm, I suspect."

"Precisely, sir," said the lad.

"We have yet to see the worst of it," said the General.

Oglethorpe led the soldier to a tent on the wind swept worksite.

"What's the cargo?"

"No cargo, sir."

"That's unfortunate." Oglethorpe shook the water from his cap and set it on a chest near the table. Settlers had been hoping for a delivery of supplies, including ale. The supplies were long over due. Oglethorpe eased himself into a chair and looked over the maps sprawled before him.

"All indentured servants," said the young man. "Forty in all — and near starvation."

Oglethorpe raised an eyebrow and turned his hawk nose up to the lad.

"Who holds their servitude?" he asked.

"The magistrate is looking into it now, sir," said the lad.

"Mr. Causton will have his hands full." He pulled a sheet of parchment from a leather satchel. "Just the same, Savannah is in need of a few good hands."

Oglethorpe dipped his pen into an inkwell and began scrawling. "Take this to Mr. Causton. Have him personally deliver it to the captain of the sloop. Tell him that I shall buy the indentures of all on board — as an act of charity, of course. Five pounds each."

"But, sir — "

Oglethorpe stopped writing. Slowly, he turned his gaze up to the soldier.

"Yes?"

"They're Irish, sir," said the lad.

The implication was obvious to the general. The charter for the trust was very clear. As England was at war with Spain (a Catholic nation), there were to be no papists allowed in the colony.

"From where do they hail?" Oglethorpe scribbled his signature on the writ.

"Ulster," said the young man.

"Mostly Protestants in Ulster, and Presbyterians at that," said the General. He sealed the letter with a few drops of wax and set his brass stamp upon it. Oglethorpe handed the note off to the young man.

"Even so, buying the servitude of a few Irish papists might violate the letter of the law, but we are here to also relieve England of the burden of those in decayed circumstances. The spirit of the law holds us to a higher standard, I should think.

"Tell Mr. Causton that those aboard are to be assigned to attend to the widows and magistrates of

Savannah. We have need for hands at Highgate and Hampstead."

The messenger turned to go.

"One more thing," said the General. "I understand that the cattleman, William Wyse on Hutchinson's Island, has taken ill and needs both a house servant and a ranch hand. If you can find a couple who is married or otherwise betrothed, be sure to send them both to Mr. Wyse, as I am sure that keeping the Trustees' cattle healthy is more than a full time responsibility, even for those in good health."

Savannah....

Rain stung Alice's back. She could feel the rivulets of rainwater running down her face and streaming off her nose. She shook her head to shake it off.

She cursed.

Shortly after the boat docked, the magistrate and a few able-bodied tithing men met the crew. Just about everyone on board was warmly welcomed and escorted to the court house at the corner of Bull Street and Bay Lane. They were given dry clothes and a hot meal. They were also given their assignments and the conditions of their servitude. Many were grateful just to be ashore, and surprised by the twenty acres of farmland allotted to them.

Alice Riley wasn't so fortunate. As she made her way toward the gangplank, she noticed the swabbie and the fat man talking with the magistrate, Thomas Causton. Before she could even present her side of the story, she was hustled up to the guardhouse on the edge of town and locked into the pillory.

And there she stood in the rain, head and hands bound to the pine-and-pitch pillory. Hunger gnawed at her belly. Her legs trembled and ached. When they buckled, the thick timber threatened to squeeze the life out of her.

Her eyes fluttered, and she found herself dreaming of Ulster, with its green rolling hills.

TAP-TAP-TAP

Alice shook herself from the doldrums and turned her stiff neck to the source of her aggravation.

"I was dreaming," she said. "Did you have to spoil it?"

Thomas Causton leaned forward. Rainwater ran off the brim of his hat.

"I could let you go on dreaming locked in the pillory," said the magistrate. "But your accuser has dropped the charges."

"How long have I been here?" she asked.

"Three days." Causton unlatched the pillory and raised the top plank. "Standard punishment for thieves and liars."

Alice rubbed her wrists and stretched her neck. She thought of all sorts of clever curses and foul epithets she could hurl at the bailiff, but thought better of it.

"Help her walk," said Causton, motioning to two tithing men. As they moved toward Johnson Square, Causton told her of her responsibility to care for William Wyse, as a requirement for fulfilling her seven-year servitude to the Trust.

"Mr. Wyse is infirmed," said Causton. "He has a sharp mind and knows his work, but he will need to be bathed and cared for. Your fiancé, Mr. White, is already on Hutchinson's Island. He will be caring for the cattle."

Oh, Richard. Alice thought it best not to tell the magistrate that their betrothal was really only in the mind of Richard White.

Hutchinson's Island, a week later....

TINK-A-LING-A-LING

Alice sat bolt upright, bleary eyed. She stumbled over to the washbasin and splashed some cool water on her face. Then, she removed the chamber pot from its cabinet.

"It's going to be a long day," she said. "The bloody sun hasn't even come up yet, and that lazy bastard already wants my attention."

TINK-A-LING-A-LING

Oh, roll over and go back to sleep, she thought, straightening her nightgown. "And let me rest in peace!"

TINK-A-LING-A-LING

Alice grabbed her housecoat and padded across the wooden floor to the master's bedroom. She hesitated for a moment, and then knocked.

"Come," came the voice.

He had been there barely a year, but William Wyse already had a reputation amongst Trustees. Early on, even before receiving his grant of land on Hutchinson's Island, he had tried to bring a prostitute over, claiming she was his daughter. London magistrates quickly saw through this and kept her in Jolly Old England. Here, in the colony of Georgia, the Trustees presumed that the honor of their wives and daughters would remain intact with Wyse on the other side of the river.

When the bailiff, Causton, received Mr. Wyse's request for a house servant, he balked, finding it ridiculous for a charity colonist to have a servant. Still, the Trustees knew they needed someone with Wyse's experience dedicated to tending the cattle on the island. Causton knew that he needed to send a woman who could take care of herself, should Wyse take too much liberty with his servant. Alice Rilcy certainly fit the bill — especially after her assault on that worthless nc'er-do-well of a sailor.

Alice peered around the corner to see William Wyse lying in his bed, illuminated by the orange glow of a bedside lantern.

"Sir?" she said.

Wyse lay in bed with a peculiar smile on his face. With a withered hand, he patted the moss-stuffed mattress. Alice shook her head, jaw agape, too afraid to speak. Wyse waved a hand, beckoning her.

"I will do no such thing!" she said, turning away.

"I think you'll find my pillow to be far more comfortable than the pillory," said Wyse.

Alice shuddered, and then closed the door.

Hutchinson's Island, six weeks later....

As Alice prepared breakfast for Wyse, she realized that she had barely seen Richard at all. Wyse had done a fine job of running the man so ragged that he had hardly the time nor the energy to see Alice, never mind spend any time with her. For the first time in her life, she felt a longing for the man.

As she ladled the grits into Wyse's bowl, she felt a wave of nausea wash over her. She dashed for the door and rushed into the yard, still in her nightgown. She braced herself on a fencepost, and threw up. It was the fourth time in as many days.

Oh, dear God, she thought. *Let it be Richard's.*

She waited for the nausea to pass, and then she returned to the house to clean up, and to serve Wyse his breakfast.

Later that morning, Wyse lay nude in his bed. Alice dipped a sponge in a bucket of water and ran it over his withered chest. She hated the smile on his face that seemed to grow with each pass of the sponge.

"Come," said Alice, pulling Wyse to the edge of the bed. "Time to wash your hair."

Wyse let his head fall over the edge of the bed. Alice grimaced. Wyse was enjoying this far too much. Her eyes fluttered as she tried to control her simmering rage.

"You're with child, aren't you?" said Wyse.

Alice went flush.

"All the signs are there," he said. "Sick every morning. Moody. High strung — even more than normal."

The brush bit hard into Wyse's scalp.

"Ow!" said Wyse, raising a shriveled hand. "Be careful, woman!"

Alice clenched her jaw.

"I've always wanted a child," said the old man. "Do you think it's mine?"

Alice trembled. Her eyes fluttered. It was all she could do to restrain herself.

Wyse chortled. "If it's a boy, we could name him *Richard*."

Alice snarled and quickly wrapped the wet towel around the old man's spindly neck. Then, she kicked the stool out from under her, straddled the bucket, and pressed her bare feet against the wooden bed frame. With a grunt, she dragged Wyse over the side of the bed and plunged his head into the bucket of filthy water. Wyse tried to struggle, but was unable to break her grip. His body dangled over the edge of the moss-covered mattress. His feet, tangled in the sheets. Alice shoved the old man's head into the bucket over and over again, cursing his name. When Wyse stopped struggling and the last of his breath bubbled to the top of the soapy water, only then did Alice slump against the wall of the cabin.

Suddenly, she was awash with panic. She stood up and dashed out of the room. She threw her day clothes onto the bed and tried to pull the drenched nightdress off her wet body. She shrieked with frustration.

As she was struggling out of the shift, Richard burst into the room. Alice recoiled with a yelp. When she saw Richard's panic-stricken face, she collapsed, bursting into tears.

Richard slowly backed out of the room. Warily, he shuffled toward Wyse's bedroom. He rounded the corner and froze at the sight of the old man's broken body dangling off the frame of the bed, his head still immersed in the wooden bucket.

Maybe he's not dead, he thought, though he knew otherwise.

Warily, he moved toward the bed. If he could just put Wyse back in the bed and clean up the room, perhaps the settlers would believe the old man had died in his sleep. They were, after all, on the island and not on the bluff. And, while other homes dotted Hutchinson's, it was not likely that her crime would be immediately discovered.

There's still hope.

He squatted next to the bucket and slowly unraveled the wet cloth from old man Wyse's throat. He heard a shuffling behind him. He turned, thinking it was Alice. When he saw two other cattlemen standing in the doorway, Richard went numb. His hopes for a new life evaporated in the murky water that drowned old man Wyse.

Savannah, eight months later....

Alice cradled her child in her arms, a beautiful baby girl with a shock of black hair.

So much time wasted.

The trial was a sorry affair. With lawyers prohibited from the colony, she and Richard had to defend themselves before a jury of *English* peers. She tried to tell them that Richard had nothing to do with the murder, that it was all her doing. The men simply laughed, so certain were they that a woman could not have strangled a man, even one as weak as old Mr. Wyse.

They actually laughed. Alice's blood boiled at the thought of her ridicule. Then, tears fell like rain at the thought of Richard.

Poor Richard. She had been told shortly after giving birth that Richard had escaped from the crude log jail, only to be captured and hanged on the spot.

The door to the ramshackle stockade flew open. Grim men rushed in and snatched the baby away from Alice. She struggled. Pleaded. Begged. The tithing men forced her arms behind her back and quickly tied her wrists. Then, they hustled her to the gallows at Percival Square where the majority of settlers gathered to witness the execution of the colony's first murderess.

Through her tear stained eyes, their leering English faces seemed grotesque and misshapen. As they guided her steps to the top of the platform, Alice wondered how much different her life would have been had she only said "yes" the first time Richard proposed.

The hood was snapped over her head, and the world went black. Alice took a deep breath. She thought of her baby. She sighed. Then, before the hangman could push her off the platform, she stepped of the edge… and was no more.

The murder of William Wyse was the first in the colony of Georgia, with Richard White being the first man, and Alice Riley, the first woman, to be executed.

Some claim that Alice still wanders Hutchinson's Island, looking for her lost child, who died shortly after the execution of Alice Riley.

René

Savannah, 1820

René stared at the rainwater streaming down the windowpane. He pawed at the light dancing through the droplets.

"René…." The voice seemed so distant.

"René!"

René shook himself out of his thousand-yard stare and gazed blankly at his father.

"Come wash up," his father said, careful not to touch the boy. René hated to be touched. "It's time for dinner."

The boy raised himself up to his full height. He towered over his father.

"Here," his father said, handing the boy a bar of soap. René stared into space.

"If you don't wash up, you won't eat!"

René let the soap fall into the washbasin. His stocky father grabbed René's hands and quickly shoved him into the wall.

Through clenched teeth, he said, "Why do you always have to make this so difficult, boy?

"If I didn't know better, I'd swear the devil's got a hold of you!"

They settled down at the dinner table. René hunched over his food. His father watched the hulking teen ravenously shovel food into his mouth with his bare hands. In his younger days, Rémy might have thought that this was some punishment for past sins, but the passing of his wife was penance enough for anyone.

René slammed his plate against the table and glared at his father.

"There's no more, son," his father said, reaching for the plate. René seized his father's hand and pinned it to the table. Without warning, his father kicked the chair out from under the boy and settled his full weight on his son.

"René," his father whispered. "Please, be calm."

Hours passed….

Rémy could hear his son sleeping soundly. Staring at the ceiling, he thought of all the towns they had passed through: New Orleans, Biloxi, Mussel Shoals, and now Savannah. In each place, he tried to make a new start, working the shipyards and the loading docks, trying to support himself and his son. He wandered back alleys in search of a treatment for whatever was ailing his son: root work, exorcism, voodoo – anything short of the horrific remedy prescribed by practitioners of so-called modern medicine.

No matter where they tried to settle, something would always go wrong, and the townsfolk would always blame René, suspicious of what they couldn't understand.

"He's a good boy," his father whispered as he drifted off to sleep. "Just... misunderstood."

Morning always comes too early. Rémy looked over at his son, still sleeping soundly. He rolled over, folded up his bedding, and tucked it neatly in the corner near the hearth. The tiny one room cottage was all they could afford – at least until he got his first week's pay. Even then, he owed the company store for the advance he received for a week's rations.

"I'll never get out of the hole," he sighed.

After breakfast, Rémy helped his son wash up.

"Good work, son!" said Rémy. "Thank you."

René smiled at his father.

"Now, René, I'll be back in a little while," he said. "Okay?"

René shook his head.

"You'll be fine, son." Rémy grabbed his cap and headed for the door. René blocked his way.

"Son, you know you can't come with me."

René puffed up his chest and leaned into his father.

"Son," said Rémy, his voice icy with resolve. "Let me pass."

René slumped his shoulders and stepped out of the way.

"Thank you."

Rémy squeezed through the doorway and headed toward the shipyards on River Street. He could hear his son's plodding footsteps following behind. Rémy stopped.

"Come on, René," he said without turning around.

The two continued on to the shipyard.

Rémy signed in and collected his tools.

"You're late," said the foreman. "You know I'll have to...."

"Dock my pay?" said Rémy. "Fine by me. Can't take nothin' from nothin'."

"Get to work." The foreman shoved the tool kit into Rémy's arms.

René sat on the riverbank, watching the light dance on the water. He could hear the sounds of slave children splashing in the water just around the bend. Eventually, he stood up and waded through the silt and mud, making his way toward the splashing and laughing. René parted the branches and watched the children splash and play. He barked out a hearty, clumsy laugh.

The playing stopped.

Laughing, René ran to join the children. He just couldn't help himself.

The young boys exchanged nervous glances as the colossal teen stumbled toward them like some monstrous toddler. They shrieked and sprinted toward the shore, disappearing into the brush.

When his laughing stopped, René looked around to find no one. He felt lonely as ever. René sat in the river, sobbing.

About that time, a mounted patroller rode up to the riverbank. Apparently, someone had reported that some boys were swimming in the river.

"Come on, son," he said. "If you get on out now, I'll pretend that I never saw you."

René just stared at the water, still sobbing.

"Come on, now," the patroller said. "If you don't come out of the water, I'm gonna have to give you the lashings!"

René barely heard the man. He just kept staring at the water.

"Come on, boy!" The patroller dismounted. Riding crop in hand, he waded in the river toward the boy.

René's heart raced. *Where's Papa?*

The patroller placed a firm hand on the boy's shoulder.

"Git up!"

The boy-giant sprang to his feet, howling. He flailed his arms about and lumbered through the muck, trying to find his father.

In his panic, René bowled the patroller over, sending him headlong into the muddy riverbank. The patroller clutched at the mud and the silt, trying to flee the giant.

"RENÉ!"

Rémy sprinted over to his wailing son, who was trying to free himself from the muck.

"Come here, son!" Rémy offered his hand. René took it, gladly. Almost immediately the boy relaxed, and eased himself onto the riverbank. Rémy lay on the grass, holding his son's hand.

"It's okay, son."

The patroller had finally climbed the banks and was all too eager to leave – but not without firing a parting shot.

"You keep that freak away from me!" the patroller cried, sloughing off the mud and silt. "You hear me?!"

Rémy simply stared at the man.

"Come on, René," he said calmly. "Let's go home."

The next morning, René awoke to an empty cottage.

Where's Papa?

René stumbled to the door. He pulled, expecting it to fly open. The door held fast.

"Papa!" he cried, pulling harder.

He slammed his fists against the door, calling for his father. Moments grew into hours.... Eventually, the boy-giant slumped against the door. His wailing eased into a soft, pitiful keening.

The boy crawled over to his bedding. Tears fell to the blanket, leaving dark blotches. With thick fingers, René tried to remove the tearstains. He believed that if he rubbed hard enough, the quilt would be like new. It had to be. Everything had to be just right. It just had to be. He couldn't put the bedding away like his father had taught until everything was just right.

But everything was wrong....

His chest tightened as he tried to erase the tearstains, but one by one, they kept appearing. René's breathing became swift and shallow. He could feel his face getting warmer — and wasn't it already hotter than a potbellied stove in that cramped cabin? *And where was Papa?*

The boy-giant snatched up the blanket and threw it down. He jumped to his feet and wheeled around. He kicked over the rough-hewn table, then seized a chair and hurled it against the door, the chair splintering on impact

René howled, then collapsed. With the rage of a teething toddler, René pounded his fists against the planked floor.

Slave children playing in Greene Square heard the wailing. They gathered near the fence facing the tiny cottage.

"Mama say he possessed," said Dembi.

"You hear that howlin'?" said Sam. "I bet he a wolf."

"Ain't no wolf," said a slender girl.

"Hush, Sable!"

"Yeah, Sable. What you know 'bout it?"

"Wolf or not," said Sable. "He must be lon'ly."

Sable pushed off the fence and began walking away from the boys.

"Sable!" said Sam. "Where you goin'?"

Sable called back without turning around.

"To see if he lon'ly."

The boys dashed over to Sable.

"You crazy?" said Dembi, blocking her way. "He tear you up!"

"If he don't, Mama will!" Sam said.

Sable kept walking toward the cabin.

"Sable!" said the boys in unison.

"All I know is we suppos' to love one another," she said. "Ain't that what the preacher said this mornin'?"

"But...."

Sable wheeled around and thrust her tiny fists on her hips. She stared at Dembi, pursing her lips.

"Oh, that's right," said Sable, her head rocking with every other word. "You wouldn't know that cuz you skipped out 'fore the sermon!"

Sam grabbed Dembi by the arm.

"Come on, Dembi!" said Sam through clenched teeth.

Dembi didn't know whether he was more afraid of Sable, his mama, or that wolf-boy howlin' in the cabin. He thought of a dozen things to say, some sharper than others. In the end, he just let her pass.

René huddled in a dark corner of the room. He embraced his knees and rocked slowly, gently, sobbing every so often. Then, something caught his attention. Through watery eyes, he could see a woolly mane rising in the window, backlit by the afternoon sun. There was a grinding of wood-on-wood, then the clatter of a plank against the earth.

The door creaked. René shielded his eyes from the daylight that flooded the room.

"You ain't no wolf," said the slender silhouette, which stood in the doorway.

Sable looked around the cramped room and shook her head.

"You jus' been havin' yourself a time in here!"

René sat motionless, still cradling his knees. Sable gathered up the pieces of the shattered chair.

"Might could fix this," she said, laying the pieces in a neat pile near the door. Then, Sable moved to the overturned table. She squatted down and grabbed the lip of the table. Sable strained, but the table was too heavy. She plopped onto the floor.

"You jus' gonna sit there?" she said, leaning against the wall. "This table ain't gonna right itself, now."

René rose to his full height. Tiny Sable's jaw dropped in astonishment. The boy-giant was easily twice as tall – at least it seemed that way to Sable.

The boy stalked over to the table. Sable scuttled like a crab toward the door and watched as the giant effortlessly lifted the heavy table and set it upright. Calmly, René regarded the crouching little girl.

"Don't you have a smile?" Sable said, dusting herself off.

René grinned broadly.

Sable looked toward the hearth and noticed the broom was resting on its bristles.

"Oh no," she said, grabbing the broom. "You can't have no broom restin' like that. It's bad for the broom, and bad for you!

"Leas' that's what Mama say." Sable started sweeping.

"Now, pay 'tention," said Sable, sweeping the dirt toward the center of the room. "You can never sweep the dirt out the do', 'less you want more bad luck. Seems to me you got plenty of that already.

"An' once you got yo'self a little pile like this here, you scoop it up, jus' like this, and carry it outside."

Sable stepped just outside the door and emptied the makeshift dustpan. Then, she came back in and set the broom upright on its handle, patting it to make sure it was secure.

"Mm-hmm," she said with satisfaction. "Oh, an' never sweep when they's company, 'less you want them to leave."

"SAY-BLE!"

Sable winced at the sound of her mama's voice.

"I got to go," she said with a shrug. Then, she hurled herself at René and wrapped her arms around his thick leg. Instead of panicking, the giant smiled, and gently placed an enormous hand on her woolly head.

"Be good!" she said, pulling away.

Sable dashed out the door. The boy shuffled to the door and watched Sable sprinting toward Greene Square, kicking up dirt as she ran.

Rémy strode down Houston Street, eager to get home to his son. It had been a trying day at the shipyard. His co-workers had heard all about his son and how the lumbering oaf beat down a patroller. Rémy did his best to explain René's condition, and how the boy was simply misunderstood, but the men at the yard kept pressing the issue. Eventually, Rémy just had to walk away.

As he returned his tools to the foreman, he heard a couple of slaves talking about the wolf-boy who lived near Fort Wayne.

"S'pose I'd howl too if I was locked up all day," one said.

"What else he go'n' do?" said another. "Can't have no devil-chil' runnin' 'bout."

He's no devil-child, Rémy thought as he shuffled through Greene Square. Up ahead, he could see the door to his cabin was wide open.

He panicked.

Rémy dropped his sack and sprinted for the door. He burst into the room and found his son sleeping peacefully, his head resting on a neatly folded quilt.

The next morning, René stood at the window, hoping his friend would stop by to see him. He never had any friends. Everyone was always afraid of him — as far as René could tell — and for no good reason. Papa was the only friend he had in the world, but he was hardly there.

Oh, he understood that Papa had to work so they could eat, and Papa did explain that his work was often dangerous and no place for a boy. Still, that didn't help.

The boy kept staring out the window, waiting for the friend that might never show. He found himself staring off into nothingness, then —

BAP!

René jumped back with a yelp. When he realized nothing was wrong, he timidly approached the glass. A tiny smudge had appeared. The boy pawed at the glass, but the smudge stayed. He cocked his head and pressed his face against the glass. A morning dove fluttered in the dirt below. René shrieked.

He seized the door handle and fully expected to find it barred. Instead, the door flew open and slammed against the side of the cabin, startling several slave children. The giant lumbered out into the street. Slave children scattered. He glanced around, looking for the bird. There below, still as the dawn, lay the dove. René plopped himself down and gathered up the dove in his massive paws. Gently, sweetly, he caressed the bird as if that would somehow bring the poor creature back to life.

Hours passed....

René sat in front of the tiny cottage holding the lifeless bird as if it were the only thing that protected him from the rest of the world. To him, it was. Throughout the day, passersby muttered to themselves, or shot him worrisome glances, but René didn't care. What mattered, to the exclusion of all else, was that bird cradled in his colossal hand.

Eventually, the hot sun got the best of René, and he sought shelter in the corner of the cabin, still clutching the bird.

Rémy stared at his beer. He knew René was waiting for him at home. The boy had been cooped up in that tiny cabin all day and was probably starved — for dinner, and for affection.

I'm trying, son.

He took a swig of his ale and caught a glimpse of his reflection in the mirror behind the bar. He was little more than thirty, but years of sleepless nights and hard labor had taken their toll. Rémy ran a calloused hand over his face, as if this would somehow smooth away the furrows of worry. Wearily, he dropped his head.

"Shouldn't you be home?" sounded a familiar voice.

Rémy slowly opened his eyes and raised his head. He regarded the gentleman through the reflection. He sighed. It was the patroller.

"We've got to stop meeting like this," said Rémy. "People will talk."

"People are talking," said the patroller, nodding toward the barkeep.

"Ain't that sump'in'." Rémy sipped his beer without looking at the young man.

"I can let it pass, what happened at the river," he said. "But every day, I hear some new story about the boy-giant and how he likes to scare children or kill small animals."

"That's not my son," said Rémy. He stood up and tossed a few coins onto the bar.

"How would you know?" said the patroller, leaning against the bar. "You're never home."

Rémy snapped the stool out from under the patroller. The young man cracked his chin against the bar and hit the floor — hard. Patrons scattered, expecting an all-out brawl.

"What's your name, boy?" Rémy loomed over the glass-jawed cop, wielding the stool like a cudgel.

"Lockley. Charles Lockley," he said, curled up against the foot rail.

"Charlie, you ain't done enough livin' to talk to me like that," said Rémy. "Not me, or anyone else."

He set the stool down, grabbed his hat, and stormed out the door.

The smoky flame sputtered to life. Satisfied with his work, the lamplighter tapped the hatch shut and moved on.

Sarge breathed a sigh of relief as the whistling lamplighter moved away from the steps to Mrs. Platt's boarding house.

Then, a knock at the door startled the crusty soldier. He pulled the stained blanket around him and shuffled over to the door.

He carefully eased himself against the doorframe, so as not to make a sound. Sarge held his breath and listened.

One man? Or two?

THUD-THUD-THUD

He jumped back.

"Sarge?" came the voice.

Sarge yanked the door open and yarded the young man into the room.

"Are you crazy?" he said through clenched teeth. "Somebody will see you!"

"But you *sent* for me," Lockley said, wide-eyed.

"Yes. And I told you to be discreet!"

Sarge moved to the window and shut the curtains. Darkness bathed the room.

"What are you doing?" said Lockley. "And what is that smell?"

Lockley struck a match and lit the lamp mounted to the wall. Slowly, his eyes adjusted to the dim light. He could see his father's war buddy huddled in a corner.

"I did a bad thing, Charlie," he said, tracing absent patterns on the wall.

Lockley took a step, then another. He stepped in something.... Something sticky, something... wet.

The patroller looked down. He found himself standing in a pool of blood. Lockley could feel the bile churning. He raced to the window and tried to open it, but Sarge seized him and threw him to the ground.

"You've got to help me, Charlie!" Sarge said, clutching Lockley's collar. Lockley turned to avoid the madman's gaze. He found himself staring into the vacant eyes of a young girl.

"She was going to ruin everything!"

Lockley struggled against the weight of the older man.

"Get off me!" he said, fighting back the nausea.

Sarge eased his grip. Lockley scuttled out from under the man, slipping on the thick blood. He crawled toward the fireplace and wretched into the cold ashes.

"S-she was so easy on the eyes, Charlie," said Sarge, leaning against the wall. "With those locks of red hair...."

"She's a girl, you pig!" Lockley said, wiping his mouth with his sleeve.

Sarge lunged at the patroller and shoved him into the ashes.

"Show some respect, boy! If it weren't for me, your father would have died in the marshes."

Lockley cursed the deathbed promise he made to his father.

"I'll help you," he said through gritted teeth.

Sarge rolled off Lockley and sagged against the brick. Lockley stood up and spit into the fireplace. He wiped his face with the soiled blanket and hurled it at Sarge.

Rémy quietly barred the door to his cottage. His son was finally sleeping. He and René had spent the better part of the night tussling over the dead bird René had found. The boy-giant refused to let go of it, so Rémy waited. And waited. Once René nodded off, he gingerly freed it from his son's huge hand.

Every once in a while, the strangest things would attract René's attention, and the boy-giant would form a strong attachment – an unnatural attachment – to the thing. Once, it was his blanket. Another time, a broom. Last night, it was the dead bird. Rémy relented most times, because giving in was easier than fighting with his son. But a dead bird was too much.

Rémy skulked toward Greene Square, cradling the dead bird in one hand, toting a spade in the other. He crawled through the fence and surveyed the square, trying to find a good place to bury the bird. In the end, he decided on digging a shallow grave near the fence post.

As the spade cut into the hard earth, a horrific scream shattered the silence. Rémy dropped the spade and sprinted toward the panicked cry. Others emerged from their cottages bearing lanterns. Pretty soon, the whole of Greene Ward, and a few folks from Columbia Ward and Carpenter's Row gathered near East Broad Street. There, shoved under a porch near York Lane lay the body of a young girl with locks of red hair.

Rémy forced his way through the crowd of crying women and cursing men. One thug grabbed him by the shoulder and wheeled him around. Rémy felt the crushing blow of a huge fist slamming into his skull. He staggered back, falling into the crowd. They held him fast.

"It's your boy what did this!" bellowed the brute. The crowd join in, their clashing voices incomprehensible.

"He was with me all night!" Rémy shouted back.

The burly Irishman grabbed him by the collar.

"Where is he now?" he said, teeth clenched.

"Sleeping."

The crowd half-carried Rémy to the door of his cabin. When they were within paces of the cottage, the Irishman shoved him. Rémy stumbled headlong, crashing into the tiny house. He watched as the crowd inspected the barred door, and stood by helplessly as the burly man yarded off the plank that held the door fast.

One by one, nosey neighbors peeked their heads into the dwelling, only to find the boy-giant sleeping peacefully. One by one, they shuffled back to the comforts of their beds.

Sarge slugged a shot of rotgut and waited in the livery stable behind Mrs. Platt's boarding house. It had been three nights since Lockley had "taken care of" the girl.

Good ol' Charlie, he thought. *Loyal, just like his dad*.

The old man took another swig as Lockley entered the stable.

"They'll be here soon," said the patroller.

"I hope so," said Sarge, squinting at his pocket watch. "It's damn near two in the mornin'."

Lockely jumped as the stable door creaked open.

"Easy lad."

Rogan, the burly Irishman, strode into the barn along with a dozen others from Greene Square and other wards. The grim men perched on hay bales and barrels, waiting for someone to speak.

"You know why you're here," said Lockley, breaking the heavy silence.

"The boy," said Rogan.

"The boy!" shouted the others.

"Keep it down!" said Sarge. "Let's not wake Mrs. Platt!"

"All I know is he's the one who kill'd that poor girl!" said Rogan.

"You see it?" asked Freeman.

"Don't have to. All the signs are there!"

"What signs?" asked Sarge.

"He's mean!" said one.

"Yeah," said Freeman. "Every day, I heah how he scare the chirrun. Scare 'em to death!"

"Charlie, weren't you assaulted by the boy?" asked Sarge.

"He hit you?" said Rogan.

"Damn near drown'd 'im," said Sarge.

"It's prob'ly nothin'," said a wiry man. "But my wife tells me she saw him torturing a small bird."

"Ain't nothin'?" said Rogan. "It proves he ain't right in the head."

"Shows he ain't got no feelings."

"Or respect."

"Why ain't you doin' somethin' 'bout it, Charlie?" asked Sarge.

"My hands are tied," said Lockley. "You know as well as I do that it'll never make it to trial. And even if it does,"

"He'll walk away, won't he?" asked Sarge.

"I say we take matters into our own hands!" said Rogan. "We all know he killed that girl."

"What if it wasn't him?" asked Freeman.

"Do you want to take that chance? What if it were your niece, Sable?"

"Yeah," said the wiry man. "Didn't I see her high-tail it outta his cabin the other day?"

"She say he harmless," said Freeman.

"Course she's gonna say that," said Sarge. "All kids lie when they're trying to avoid the switch."

The men nodded.

"When?" said Lockley. "I can't be around when it happens."

"Tonight. Now!" said Rogan.

"Patrol along Jackson Ward tonight," said Sarge.

"Go!" said Rogan. "We'll give you a head start!"

Lockley's heart raced. He grabbed his lantern and strode out the door. In the stable, the men gathered the tools for their murderous scheme: shovels, pitchforks, a burlap sack, a length of rope. They passed around oil-soaked torches and lit them using Sarge's lantern. The hard-faced men exchanged grim glances. Then, like wild dogs, they slinked into the darkness. As they filed out the door, their torches dripped smoldering scraps onto the straw floor.

The door to the cottage burst open. René shrieked. The men barged into the tiny room. Rémy jumped to his feet and cold-cocked the wiry man. Two others rushed him, forcing him up against the wall as the burly Irishman drove his fist into Rémy's gut again and again. With a vicious hook to the head, Rémy tumbled to the floor.

René howled. The wiry man sprinted out the door. The remaining men snapped their gazes over to the corner where the boy-giant huddled, wide-eyed, clutching his blanket.

"Hold, now. He ain't no killer," said Freeman. "He just a boy."

Rogan leaned into Freeman. "You ain't havin' second thoughts, are ya?"

"I know I can't stop you," said Freeman. "But I sho' ain't goin' ta help you neither."

Freeman dropped his pitchfork and shuffled out the door.

"Anybody else?" growled the burly man. Hearing no objections, Rogan tossed the sack to a stocky dockworker.

René frantically flailed his hands about, trying desperately to fend off the men. One tried to grab René by the collar of the boy's nightshirt. René shrieked and gave the man a powerful shove, sending him into the crowd of cronies. Then, rather than trying to flee his attackers, René curled up into a ball and tried to hide under the blanket.

"Forget the bag," said Rogan. "Use the blanket instead."

Quickly, the men lashed René's legs together. They tied the blanket around the boy's head and strapped his hands together.

"Just like a hog," Rogan snickered.

The men grunted as they lifted the boy.

"He's gotta weigh about 400," said one.

"At least," grumbled another.

The men shuffled through Greene Square down

Dounton Street and past the slave dwellings. Occasionally, they'd shrug to get a better grip on the ties binding the boy-giant.

"Why ain't he fightin'?" said one.

"Too scared," said another. "He just pissed himself."

The men laughed.

Soon, the men found themselves slogging through shallow water where the rice paddies met the marsh. René's heavy body pushed the men deeper into the muck.

Rogan trudged over to a gnarled oak and tossed the noose over the thick branch. Then, he slogged through the muck and slipped the noose over the boy's head. René sobbed, though the quilt muffled his cry.

"Heave!" shouted Rogan.

The men dropped the boy in the marsh and seized the rope. They leaned hard, struggling to get the boy off the ground. A couple of men fell into the water, and the boy-giant dropped. The rope bit into the tree, and snapped taught.

"Lean!" Rogan growled.

The men strained against the weight of the boy. It took all ten men to heave the boy off the ground – and only then did René struggle.

Wiry stumbled down the hill.

"FIRE!" he shouted.

The men looked up, startled.

"What in the hell are you doing?" said Rogan.

"The whole city is burning down!" Wiry said, gesturing toward the west. "Look!"

An orange glow blanketed the sky.

Back at the cabin, Rémy struggled to his feet. His head throbbed.

"FIRE!" came the cries of the panicked.

Let it burn, he thought as he leaned against the doorframe.

Freeman came running across the square. Rémy could only see red. He dashed across the square and tackled the man.

"Hold up! Hold up!" said Freeman, trying to protect himself from the threatening blow. "I know where he is!"

Rémy lifted the man up by his collar.

"If my boy is dead," he growled.

"You keep talkin', he ain't gonna make it!"

Freeman and Rémy dashed through Greene Square. The ward was deserted. Everyone had gone to battle the blaze.

Down the hill they stumbled. They splashed through the rice fields and slogged through the muck. There, silhouetted against the hellish sky, was René, swinging from the oak.

Rémy mouthed his son's name, but could make no sound.

"RÉMY!" called Freeman, sawing through the thick rope.

Rémy shook it off and trudged through the muck, sobbing. He grabbed his son's legs and held them tight to his chest.

SNAP!

René crashed to the ground. The boggy earth braced his fall. Frantically, Rémy worked to free his son from the suffocating bonds while Freeman untied the boy's legs. Tears streamed down Rémy's face as he ripped the quilt from the boy's head and leaned over his son's mouth to check his breathing.

Sobbing, Rémy cradled his son long into the morning.

If you travel up and down the East Coast, you will find several variations of this story. In Charleston, for example, he is called René Vondolla. In every "account" but this, the boy giant has always been described as a murderous monster. I always saw him as misunderstood; the monster is us.

It is interesting to note the incredible similarities between the various René tales, even across state lines. "René" in any of its variations is one of those legends that takes root in the psyche. The legend seems to resist the naysayer. In fact, the harder one tries to debunk it as myth or legend, the more fervently people cling to it. It makes one wonder why, to this day, some life-long residents swear that the boy-giant still wanders the streets of the area once called Foley's Alley. After all, they say, his remains were never found....

Dreadful Pestilence

The Diary of Marie Russell

September 20, 1979 — After months of renting, we finally closed on our house! It is so beautiful. I'm told that it took months to move from Lazaretto Creek to this quiet patch of land and that the house used to be two stories (it's now a story and a half). Still, we couldn't be happier. I am looking forward to settling in, and enjoying long, summer evenings on the front porch with my husband, Joe.

October 1, 1979 — My nephew left shortly after breakfast. He was supposed to help us with some of the painting. He tells me that, around two in the morning, he felt someone touch his foot while he slept, and then felt a cool hand touch his forehead. We awoke to find him sleeping on the floor at the foot of our bed. Whatever it was, it sure scared the wits out of him. I hope he comes back to visit....

October 8, 1979 — I'm now convinced that the home is haunted. I heard a noise that sounded like someone was making breakfast in our kitchen! I tried to wake Joe, but he told me to go back to sleep. Typical! He said he didn't hear anything — but I did! I threw on my robe and went down to the kitchen. You know how they say "fight or flight?" When I saw that young woman in the white dress standing in my kitchen, I froze. I couldn't even scream. Joe doesn't believe me, but I saw her! She had long hair, and it looked like she was carrying a large basin. Maybe she was a nurse. I don't know. But I do remember what she told me. "I have to stay here until they all get well...." What I really don't get is why these strange things keep happening at 2:14 A.M.?

The Journal of
Dr. Ernst Schreiber

14 September 1820 — I fear I have no spirit left in me. That which was not left at bedside in Carpenter's Row (on the edge of Washington Ward) was surely drained as I wandered through these barren streets.

The emptiness of the city is disquieting. Anyone of means has abandoned their homes and this city. They do so with no shame, as this pestilence has cast its dreadful pall across every ward. Save those tireless practitioners of the medical arts such as Drs. Waring, Berrien (whom I must visit before retiring, as he, himself, has exhibited symptoms), and Dr. Mary Lavinder (the obstetrician), only Negroes and the destitute remain….

14 September, The Berrien Residence — Dr. Berrien and I have differing opinions of how to treat this fever and, despite his ghastly appearance (his jaundiced skin, the scleral irritation causing horrifically bloodshot eyes, and a thrush-coated tongue, thick with what must be *Candida albicans*), he absolutely insists that I not use my lancets. I tried to reason with him (his pulse was racing and I desperately needed to lower his blood pressure), but the doctor insisted on being immersed in cool water and treated with the dried root bark of the sassafras tree. He also refused the accepted practice of puking and purging, and instead asked me to make him a poultice made primarily of lemongrass. Were he not such a respected physician, I would think this ague had driven him to a state of delirium. Dr. Berrien was kind enough to provide me with instructions (as best he could), and I shall record these in a separate journal — for posterity's sake, of course.

While I certainly said nothing to Mrs. Berrien, I fear that we are merely providing more comfort than aid, as he must surely be in his last days.

15 September, The Bulloch Residence — Mayor Charlton has finally admitted this is something

more than "fever and ague." I had wondered why the City had taken so long to advise the citizenry to abandon this dreadful place. (Secretly, I wondered whether the Board of Health wasn't somehow involved in this conspiracy to hide the truth from Savannahians. I certainly know that City Council had long been filing false reports as to the general well being of the city. Could they not see the epidemic proportions of the dead and dying? Such is the morass of politics.)

The mayor in his proclamation declared that it is "prudent for any person... to remove beyond the limits of the city's atmosphere." Indeed. The very air is poison. The fire earlier in the year has exposed cellars and vaults, which are now filled with stagnant water. I shouldn't wonder whether the fungus, mold, and algae aren't contributing to the miasma that hangs over the city.

Dr. Waring has advised City Council to instruct its scavengers to step up their work, removing the carcasses of animals, and sweeping all pools of standing water. Negroes have been commissioned to load the dead onto carts and wheel them over to an already overflowing cemetery. Sadly, there will be no time for proper burials, and no family to stand over the graves even if we had such luxury. Paupers' graves for all, I fear. A close friend of Mayor Charlton tells me that members of the clergy have been brought into the city, not for last rites or vespers, but to consecrate more ground for burying the dead.

My good friend, William Bulloch, in whose house I stay while I care for the victims, has said that few will escape this Dreadful Pestilence. He penned in a letter to a mutual friend words so eloquently written, I dare not attempt to paraphrase. "It is a harrowing task to recount the affliction of our deserted and ill-fated city."

Indeed. This fever does not discriminate between the ages, the sexes, or the races. Even the Negroes, whose African blood is supposed to impart some natural immunity, have fallen victim. Sadly, those without means will, as they always will, suffer the greatest. They can only pray that the sickly season will end before it claims another of their beloved.

20 September, The Bulloch Residence — This morning, without the benefit of my morning tea, I was called to the squalid hovel of a mechanic on Carpenter's Row. There was nothing I could do, except pronounce his death. His continued fever had lasted four days, so says his young daughter (who had also exhibited early symptoms. I prescribed bed rest and shall attempt to bleed her later this day). By the time I arrived (again, not being informed of his condition until the fourth day), the

man was already hemorrhaging steadily from the nose and bowels. His gums were soft, almost spongy. Dr. Waring notes — and I agree; surely, with the black vomit and hemorrhaging from the bowels, the constant of this disease is the stomach, and it is there where the core of the malady surely resides. I shall step up the use of emetics and laxatives. (The use of turpentine has proved to be an irritant. For now, a dose of tar mixed with water should suffice....)

A few houses down, another family begged me to treat their young boy. They tell me he woke that morning, feeling "right as rain." He dressed and left the house, only to collapse just outside their door. He is resting peacefully now, though his family will never again know the joy of his company.

Why do these people wait so long to inform us of their maladies? Don't they know that treatment in the earliest stages of this pestilence could very well prevent a needless death?

20 September, The Berrien Residence — With heavy hand, I write of the passing of Dr. Richard M. Berrien. In a separate journal, I have recorded the dreadful means of his passing, as I do not wish to reflect on this here. No. Instead, I write of the courage of his dear wife, Elizabeth.

I approached the Berrien home and was about to knock when my heart stopped. A crepe ribbon of black had been tied to the doorknocker. I knew then that Dr. Berrien had passed. I knocked, and was greeted by a servant. Her melancholy countenance confirmed my fears. Though dressed in black, the young mulatto had draped herself in a shawl or stole made from a cloth the Negroes call *adinkra*, or some such thing. (Surely, to Western eyes like mine, the red-orange color of the fabric is wholly inappropriate during a time of loss, though I am told that, to the Africans, this is the color of mourning.) She lowered her eyes and gestured silently to the stairs leading to the master bedroom.

I laid a hand upon the banister. As I gazed upon the crepe-draped pictures of the Berrien family, I suddenly felt the cold wash of death carry over me. Drained of my courage, I bowed my head and asked God for strength, as I surely did not wish to ascend the stairs.

One heavy step after another led me to the chamber door. Mrs. Berrien must have heard my approach, for as I was about to knock, she bade me enter.

I gently pushed open the door and found Elizabeth sitting quietly by the bed, her husband's body lying in state, already washed and wrapped. The bed had been pulled into the center of the room, and I noticed that the windows all were open. I was grateful, as this September evening was particularly warm and humid, and the breeze that parted the gauzy curtains was most welcome.

Unable to find the words for my failure to cure the Doctor of this disease, I looked to his wife. She seemed at peace with his passing, though I suspect she was putting on a brave face for my benefit. Mrs. Berrien seemed to be busying herself with something. I looked to her hands and noticed that she had taken a lock of his hair and was tatting it into a rather delicate flower. (The Africans find this practice to be quite barbaric, but those of us of European descent find it to be a fitting memorial, since the hair survives the body long after death — as do the reminiscences of our beloved.)

"I shall add this to the wreath," she said, nodding to the bedside table, upon which sat a rectangular box covered with a pane of glass. Nestled inside were other delicate flowers, all tatted with locks of hair from the departed.

I pulled up a chair and sat quietly on the other side of the bed, watching her weave a lifetime of memories into this one, tiny souvenir.

21 September, The Bulloch Residence — Tonight, on my return from the wake at the Berrien Residence, I passed a Negro who was pushing a cart overflowing with the blackened corpses of an entire family that had not the resources to leave the city. I inquired as to his destination. He in-

formed me that they were to be transported to the hospital so that Dr. Waring may perform an autopsy. The African spat and muttered something about blasphemy and the desecration of the body. Poor, misguided fool! Dr. Waring's work is essential to our common cause! We would certainly never find a cure for this disease if we subscribe to their simplistic burial practices, or gave in to the superstitions that plague their kind. Why, if we were to immediately bury the dead without a proper wake, we may find ourselves interring the dead prematurely. Already, I have heard horrific reports of indigent fever victims (who, of grim necessity, were dropped into a mass grave) coming to life as the first shovelful of dirt rained down upon them. Imagine the horror of waking only to find that you lie naked with the dead! I shudder to think how many other hapless souls awoke from their stupor only to find themselves cocooned in a pine box deep below the surface. How could anyone hear their cries for help?

30 September, The Bulloch Residence — My presence has been requested elsewhere. Though there has been no evidence to show that this virus is communicable, the *New York Doctrine* still prevails. New cases of yellow fever have been noted at the quarantine facility on Lazaretto Creek near Tybee. (Fitting name, *lazaretto*. Literally, it means,

"pest house.") I'm told that the House's most experienced nurse has shown the early symptoms of muscle aches and low-grade fever, though this may be due to exhaustion. I am to board a small sailing vessel straight away. The ship will transport me directly to the Lazaretto House, as such is the only access to the quarantine facility.

30 September, Aboard *The Graben* — To look upon the waters of the Savannah River, with the early light glinting off the water and the breeze dancing gently over the marshes, one almost forgets the misery caused by this pestilence.

The crew of this small fishing vessel seems to be aware of the horror that grips Georgia's First City, though I can tell they themselves have not laid eyes upon hellish scenes that continue to haunt *my* dreams: the burning tar barrels, which fill the air with thick, acrid smoke; the corpse laden carts, weaving a twisted path for the wailing and the keening to follow; the barren streets; the burned out buildings; the broken bodies. Surely, we wander through a level of Hell unfathomable even by Dante. (I shamefully admit that, in quieter moments, I afford myself the luxury of wondering what atrocities these Savannahians could have committed to merit such damnation ahead of the grave. I pray for their salvation.)

01 October, The Lazaretto House — I am much relieved to be away from the city. This morning, I

took my tea on the veranda. Sunrise has painted this white house a brilliant orange. I take a moment to listen to the marsh. Apart from the flapping of a crane's wings, all is quiet. It is hard to believe that only yesterday, I was surrounded by death.

Behind the doors to this house, another kind of misery awaits. Most have simple diseases (compared to the Black Vomit), like scurvy, brought on by malnutrition from months at sea. Others have digestive maladies, such as dysentery, and cannot be released from this house until they are well. (Having treated so many victims of the Black Vomit, I was understandably alarmed when patients here exhibited similar symptoms: inflammation, fever, chills, severe diarrhea with the passage of blood and mucous. However, unlike yellow fever, a strict regimen of water and re-hydration salts will usually save a patient — at least from dysentery.)

The facility's doctor was, himself, overcome by yellow fever in September, and was hastily buried in a nearby grave with no marker (thus, the reason for the request of my presence). The faithful nurse, while capable (having had more field experience than some of my colleagues), is over-worked — if not overwhelmed. I tried to convince her to take leave of this place, so that she may recover. She promptly declined. Her words to me demonstrated an uncommon valor, and inspired a melancholy sentiment as to the uncertainty of life itself: "I must stay until they either get well, or we all die."

02 October — I have requested that another nurse (and perhaps another physician) be sent to the Lazaretto House. Miss Eliza (James, the attending nurse) collapsed while making her rounds. Her pulse is racing — well over 100 beats per minute. Despite her objections, I have quarantined her from the rest of the infirmed.

In her weakened state, I dare not risk any new infection that might impede her recovery. Therefore, I have ruled out the use of lancets in bleeding, and will instead employ leeches. Fortunately, the staff here has done an excellent job of maintaining a healthy leech jar.

03 October — Protocol dictates that I shall not induce vomiting or prescribe emetics in this environment. As I am only one man fighting a variety of diseases, I have little time to properly dispose of human waste in a sanitary fashion — though I must. On average, I am averaging perhaps four hours sleep per night. I shouldn't wonder whether my judgment is failing me....

Miss Eliza tells me she is in better spirits, though I refuse to release her from her bed. She must rest if she is to recover. I *need* her to recover.

04 October — After completion of my rounds, I visited Miss Eliza and was disheartened by what I witnessed: she had taken a lock of her own beautiful hair and had begun tatting it in the same fashion as Mrs. Berrien. I implored her to take heart! It was then — lacking the strength to speak — that she silently directed me to look under the sick bed. With trembling hand, I lifted the bed sheet, only to find my worst fears confirmed: her chamber pot was filled with the black vomit! I forged a stiff upper lip and removed myself to dispose of her waste — and to brace myself for her inevitable passing.

06 October — Sleep has become a guilty pleasure, interrupted by nightmarish remembrances. Despite the risk to my own health, I now nap with my door open so that I may listen for any disturbances in the night. (Miss Eliza rests in the room next to mine.)

I thought perhaps I heard a stirring, and found myself wandering the house, hoping to exhaust the body that the mind will not let rest. From the main room, where the sailors rest, I heard a staccato rapping coming from Eliza's room. I rushed to her aid, only to find her in the throes of a seizure! Quickly, I threw myself over her (to keep her from injuring herself) and waited until the tremors ceased....

07 October — Miss Eliza has no recollection of her seizures last night. It is for the best, I suppose, though I am sure the telltale bruising provides all the evidence she needs. She continues to tat the lock of her long, beautiful hair and now seems ready to embrace death. It is as if each moment of her life is captured in a strand of hair, and is forever filed away with each delicate stitch.

08 October — Miss Eliza James, faithful nurse who aided the infirmed at the Lazaretto House near Tybee Island, expired. Her time of death: 2:14 AM. I have not the words to describe my sorrow....

By the time winter came to Savannah, nearly 700 people succumbed to the Dreadful Pestilence, most buried at Colonial Cemetery. It would be another eighty years before the culprit and carrier, Aedes aegypti — *the mosquito — would be found.*

Dr. James Waring, son of William, would pick up his father's work in 1876, when the disease would strike again. (Another outbreak occurred in 1854.) In all, if Dr. William Waring's estimates were correct, more than 5,000 Savannahians died of yellow fever over a span of seven decades — from 1807 to 1876. In essence, the numerical population of Savannah (of 5,000) was wiped out every fourteen years.

The Lazaretto House mentioned in this story now sits just off Highway 17, just south of Savannah. Other houses served as "Pest Houses" in times of need, though many were lost to the ravages of time and change.

A Fashionable Murder

January 1833

Robert Charlton parted the blinds of the court-house and peered out the window. A small crowd was gathering in Wright Square. He let the blinds fall and reached in his vest pocket for his watch. With a quick jerk, the face swung open. Charlton pursed his lips and snapped the watch shut. He exhaled slowly and slid the watch back in his vest pocket.

"Should be any time now," he said. Almost simultaneously the other members of the defense team looked up from their dossiers, but just as quickly returned to their writing. If the case went south, they were ready to file an appeal.

Their client, Dr. Philip Minis, stared vacantly at his hands. He had held that posture since Judge Charles Dougherty gave his "lucid and impartial charge" to the jury.

He wondered, how had he, a prominent doctor and respected member of Georgia's First City, allowed a drunken braggart to get the best of him? He found it all so hard to believe that it all began with a simple game of quoits….

Spring 1832, Luddington's Pub

James Jones Stark wedged his way between the barflies holding court. Apart from exchanging perturbed glances, the men simply shrugged and took their conversation in another part of the bar. They knew better than to argue with a man who was known for his hot temper as much as he was known for toting a pig-sticker.

The barkeep set the glass of whiskey in front of Stark. Just as he was bringing the glass to his lips, he felt a firm slap on the back. Were his elbows not firmly wedged on the bar, he might have taken a swing at the gent. Instead, he calmly set down the glass and slowly looked over his shoulder.

"Wayne," said Stark. "You ought a know better than to sneak up on a man like that."

"Who said I was sneaking?" said Wayne, motioning to the barkeep. "Everyone here saw me make a bee-line toward you."

Wayne took the glass and gestured for a toast. The two men clinked glasses and downed the shot. They grimaced. As the glasses hit the bar, they exhaled and motioned for another.

"Quoits, huhn?" said Wayne with a smirk.

"You hush," Stark said, pursing his lips.

"I reckon that might have been the greatest ass-whoopin' in the history of the game," said Wayne. "Hell, I'm surprised you showed your face in here!"

"Ain't nothin'," said Stark. "That Minis is a damned Jew."

"Well, that 'damned Jew' schooled you at the Coits Club," said Wayne. "That's for sure."

Stark tossed back another shot as applause filled the room. He looked up to see Dr. Minis enter the room to a hail of handshakes and backslapping.

"Well, James?" said Wayne, grinning from ear to ear. "Are you going to offer your heartfelt congratulations?"

Stark slammed the glass down on the bar and wiped his mouth with his sleeve. "He ought to be pissed upon."

With that, James Jones Stark straightened his coat as best he could and ploughed his way through the crowd. Everyone expected fisticuffs. Instead, Dr. Minis calmly smiled and extended his hand. Stark refused the gesture and returned it with a menacing glare. As Stark staggered onto the street, he brushed against Dr. Arnold, who was waiting to congratulate Minis on his victory. Stark grabbed Arnold by the collar and jerked a thumb in Minis's direction.

"He ain't nothin' but a damned Jew," slurred Stark.

When Dr. Arnold finally reached Minis, he placed a hand on his good friend's shoulder and said, "Do you know what Stark is saying about you?"

"I can only imagine," said Minis, forcing a smile. "And I also imagine the spirits are doing all the talking. It's nothing but the ranting of a sore loser."

July 1832, The Owens House

Parties at the Owens House always made Stark feel like royalty. It didn't matter to him that it wasn't his house, his hooch or his smokes. After a couple of belts of the good stuff and a puff or two on a big ol' stogie, Stark was living the high life.

A slender servant worked her way through the crowd. In her arms, she carried a handcrafted cedar box. Stark waved her over. She bowed her head, and then curtsied. Stark cradled her chin in his hand, encouraging her to look up at him. Instead, she shyly turned her gaze away and opened the box for him. Stark smiled and hastily selected a fat candela. He nodded his thanks as she walked away.

Stark bit off the end of his cigar and looked around for a suitable place to spit. Finding none, he waded through the tightly packed parlor to the main entrance. He opened the heavy wooden doors, leaned out and spit the soggy tobacco over the railing. Then, he lifted the glass globe from the hurricane lantern near the door and lit the torpedo with a few quick puffs.

He stepped out onto the portico. Though the night air was sultry, it was a refreshing change from the stuffy atmosphere in the parlor. As Stark pulled the door closed, he felt it tugged from his grip. He turned around to see Dr. Arnold.

"Mr. Stark," said the doctor, packing his pipe. "Mind if I join you?"

Stark puffed on his cigar.

"Beautiful night," said Arnold, "Can you imagine, the Marquis de Lafayette stood on this very spot, not ten years ago?"

"It wasn't here," said Stark, frustrated by the fraying edge of an otherwise fine cigar. "It was from the side gallery."

"Still...."

Dr. Arnold leaned against the rail and struck a small wooden match on the underside of the balustrade. It sparked and sputtered to life. Stark leaned away from the pyrotechnic display.

"Fascinating things, these matches," said Arnold, firing up his pipe. "A friend of mine brought them from Germany. They only work about half the time, and I've already burned my fingers a time or two, but there's something to be said for the convenience."

Stark gazed at the starlit sky. Arnold regarded him coolly, and then turned his gaze skyward.

"This business between you and Dr. Minis," said Dr. Arnold. "Did you ever apologize for the remark you made back at Luddington's?"

"Why would I want to do that?" said Stark leaning hard on the rail. He was now chewing on his stogie more than he was puffing. The torpedo had burned out shortly after Arnold lit his pipe. "Apologizin' ain't gonna change my opinion of the man."

"But certainly you'd agree that such scurrilous speech would call into question a man's honor," said Arnold.

"Yes, sir," said Stark, eyeing Arnold. "Provided he had any honor to begin with. Know what else?"

Arnold raised his eyebrows.

"He ain't worth the powder and shot it would take to kill him."

July 1832, Coits Club, on the Outskirts of Savannah

The iron ring bounced once in the sand and then rested on the metal stake. A second ring followed in short order. This time, the inside lip caught the stake and the ring wobbled downward, to a comfortable rest on the first.

Dr. Minis dusted his hands while Dr. Arnold and Charles Spalding applauded.

"Well, Philip," said Dr. Arnold, "I dare say you have the steadiest hands in all of Savannah."

"It's not over yet," said Spalding. He held up a metal ring and eyed the stake, several paces away.

"Come now, Mr. Spalding. You'd have to get three ringers in a row just to tie the good doctor," said Arnold.

Spalding ceased the swaying movement of his arm to glare at Dr. Arnold. Arnold replied by holding his hands up in a gesture of mock-defense. As Spalding resumed the warm up to his pitch, Arnold blustered a cough. Minis tried to conceal his grin with a forced, thoughtful expression. Spalding found himself grinning as he launched the ring.

It hooked, and bounced into the grass.

"The hell with it," said Spalding. "Good show, gents. Well played."

The men gathered their belongings and walked to the carriage. Dr. Arnold held the coat for Dr. Minis as he rolled down his sleeves.

"I saw our good friend, Stark, last night," said Arnold.

"At the party at the Owens House?"

"Yes," said Arnold. "He's still pretty upset over his loss."

"Come now," said Minis, tugging sharply on his crisp sleeve. "I find that hard to believe."

"Well, I believe it to be true," said Arnold. "Especially since he has still offered no apology for slandering your good name."

"Richard," said Dr. Minis, fastening his cuffs. "I do believe I told you that his words were induced by a night of hard drinking and a stiff, red neck."

"Perhaps," said Dr. Arnold, offering the coat for Dr. Minis. "But if a man were to insult not only my good name, but the reputation of my ancestors, and of my race...."

"I've let this go," said Dr. Minis, shrugging into his coat. "Perhaps you should, too."

"Philip," said the doctor, holding the door to the carriage. "You should at least demand an apology, if not satisfaction. Word is spreading that you are a man without honor — and a coward. I should think you would have a vested interest in such an affair."

Dr. Minis stepped onto the runner of the carriage, but stopped for a moment to address his friend and colleague.

"Dr. Arnold, I shall request from Mr. Stark that satisfaction which one gentleman should afford another." He looked to Charles Spalding.

"And I would ask that you, Mr. Spalding, my dear friend, deliver it on my behalf." He turned his gaze back to Dr. Arnold.

"But, honestly, Richard, this is, to quote the Great Bard, 'much ado about nothing.'"

August 9, 1832, the Offices of Dr. Philip Minis

A knock at the door called Dr. Minis away from his writing. He sprinkled a little desiccant onto the pages of his ledger, and closed the heavy book.

"Come."

Dr. Minis looked up as Charles Spalding entered the room. He rose to greet his old friend.

"Charles, what a pleasant surprise!" The doctor extended a hand across the desk. After a quick hand-shake, Charles reached in his breast pocket and pulled a sealed letter.

"What is this?" asked Dr. Minis.

"Mr. Stark responded to your request." Dr. Minis took the letter from Mr. Spalding. He opened the drawer to his desk, removed a silver letter opener, and used it to break the seal. Minis chuckled.

"Sir?"

"Is he serious?" asked the doctor, easing into his high-backed chair.

"Quite serious," said Mr. Spalding.

"Rifles? Today at 5?" Dr. Minis looked over his reading glasses at the grandfather clock.

"Yes," said Spalding, checking his pocket watch against the clock. "And it's already noon."

"Such an awkward weapon for a duel, I should think." Minis pulled a sheet of parchment from his desk drawer and laid it upon the felt. He removed the cap from his inkwell and dipped his tortoise shell pen into the ink.

"Give this to Mr. Wayne. He is Mr. Stark's second, is he not?"

"He is, sir."

Minis pinched a little sodium calcium powder and sprinkled it onto the parchment. He turned in his chair and carefully blew the desiccant across the page. He leaned over his desk and folded the paper. The doctor reached in his desk drawer, removed a wax stick and waved it over the flickering flame of his desk lamp until it was just starting to melt. He carefully pressed it onto the folded parchment, and sealed it by pressing the wax with a brass stamp. Then he rose and handed the letter to Mr. Spalding.

August 9, 1832, the Residence of Thomas M. Wayne

"I don't care that his rifle is at the gunsmiths," said Mr. Wayne. "According to the Code Duello, Dr. Minis must abide by the time and place set by the challenged, in this case, Mr. Stark."

"The code also states, quite clearly, that the challenger has first right of refusal." Mr. Spalding turned for the door. As he reached the door handle, he said, "Any time tomorrow is suitable for myself and for Dr. Minis."

August 9, 1832, Screven's Ferry, South Carolina

Stark and Wayne trudged up the short hill to the bluff overlooking the Back River. Over the scattered trees on Hutchinson Island, they could make out the Savannah skyline. Though it was just after five, the sun had hours to go before setting.

"Did you tell Dr. Minis that I had an extra rifle for him?" said Stark. He funneled gunpowder down the rifle's barrel.

"It wasn't in my instructions to do so," said Wayne, handing Stark a musket ball. "But he did say he'd meet us tomorrow."

"And tomorrow, and tomorrow, and tomorrow...." Stark drove the musket ball home with a quick thrust of the ramrod.

The men nodded. Stark brought his rifle to bear on the absent Dr. Minis, and fired a volley into thin air. Then, he cradled the rifled and looked to his friend.

"Shall we?"

August 9, 1832, Burrough's Counting Room

Dr. Minis and Mr. Cohen stepped onto Bull Street.

"Do you really think they went to Screvens Ferry?" asked Cohen.

"Why should I care?" said Minis. "I responded to his articles in good faith. I trust he'll respond in kind."

"Perhaps you give him too much credit, my friend."

As the men wandered through Johnson Square discussing the day's events, they heard Dr. Arnold's voice call from East Bryan Street.

"Gentlemen! Shall we put away the day with a pint at the City Hotel?"

The men all shook hands.

"It has been a rather long day," said Dr. Minis. "I suppose one pint wouldn't do any harm."

"I'd been meaning to go there, anyway," said Mr. Cohen. "My wife keeps talking about Mr. Audubon's new book. She says I simply must acquire a copy for her."

"Fancies birds, does she?" asked Dr. Arnold.

"Yes," said Cohen. "And since Mr. Audubon is staying at the hotel...."

"I hear he is autographing copies," said Dr. Minis.

As they rounded the corner onto Bay Street, Minis nearly ran headlong into Stark. Cohen and Arnold exchanged nervous glances as Stark glared hard at coolly composed Minis. Wayne hustled over just as Stark reached for the blade tucked in his belt. He placed firm hands on Stark's arms and guided him away from the men.

Minis, Cohen, and Arnold watched as Wayne rushed Stark down Bull Street; his angry words lingered in Johnson Square.

"Let me go back and whip the damned rascal!"

Dr. Minis removed his top hat and smoothed his hair with a steady hand.

"Gentlemen?"

As they resumed their walk down Bay Street, toward the City Hotel, Dr. Arnold leaned into Dr. Minis.

"Philip, I feel that you should not act solely on the defensive. I fear for your reputation, and for your very life!"

"Tomorrow, Richard," said Minis. "It all ends tomorrow."

August 10, 1832, City Hotel

The City Hotel had a reputation as a rough-and-tumble place. From the soldier to the scallywag, young men — all with something to prove — seemed to gravitate to the bar of the City Hotel; and more than one "sporting debate" ended with pistols-at-paces, the duels taking place on the other side of the Savannah River. Therefore, it was no accident that Dr. Minis chose to meet Stark in the barroom of the hotel. Still, the weight of the pistol was of little comfort to Minis.

"Easy now," he thought. *We're just having words.*

Mr. Spalding held the door for Minis. As he entered the lobby, Minis unbuttoned his coat to allow for a quick draw, should his last attempt at diplomacy fail.

"Charles, wait here. I'll inquire as to Mr. Stark's whereabouts with the manager."

"Phillip...." Spalding grabbed Minis by the arm. Minis turned and glared at his second. Spalding relaxed his grip, but kept his steely gaze focused on the doctor.

"It has to be this way, Charles," said Minis, staring off into space. He jerked his arm out of Spalding's hand. "I'm tired of running."

"Shall I meet you in the bar?" said Spalding. Minis turned on his heel and, with a dismissive wave, stalked toward the stairs.

Spalding watched as Dr. Minis moved through the lobby. He threw a shilling or two at the paperboy, and busied himself with a quick browse through the paper. Barely a page into his reading, Spalding saw Minis stride around the corner.

"Mr. Mann informs me that Mr. Stark and Mr. Wayne are upstairs."

"Are we meeting them there, then?"

"No," said Minis. "I've asked him to invite them downstairs to join us for a drink."

The men strode through the main room and settled in the bar. Minis barely noticed the crowd of men and women gathered in the lobby, and it was just as well. He had to stay focused. He was taking a chance in calling Stark out in a public place; given the man's tendencies toward belligerence, one misstep would certainly end in tragedy. Still, Minis felt this was a calculated risk. At least he would be on record, in the public's mind, anyway, as a man who is willing to defend his honor.

Several minutes passed. Spalding thrust his nose back in the evening paper. Minis kept a wayward eye on the door, and one hand resting comfortably on the caplock. Just when Minis was about to check in again with the concierge, he heard Stark and Wayne coming down the stairs. Stark was hard to ignore, as he was already bragging about how he would beat some sense into Minis once he laid eyes on him.

Minis stepped through the door, his heart racing. He drew a sharp breath. Before Stark could reach the last step, the doctor declared in a voice loud enough for all in the room to hear, "I pronounce thee, James Jones Stark, a coward!"

Stark reached in his coat and rushed toward Minis. Minis, in one smooth motion, drew his pistol, cocked the hammer, and fired. Stark was practically on top of Minis when the cap finally ignited the powder. The bullet ripped through his chest and shot across the room, slamming into the kitchen door.

The report from the pistol rattled drinking glasses. Men and women scrambled to safety, some stumbling onto Bay Street. Spalding tossed his paper in the air and fought the panicked crowd. By the time he reached Minis, Wayne was trying to wrest the pistol from the grip of the doctor.

Doctors Waring and Arnold had heard the pandemonium from the mayor's office across the street. They rushed over to the City Hotel. Earlier in the day, Dr. Waring urged members of the Anti-dueling Association to mediate this growing dispute between Stark and Minis, and now Dr. Waring knew they were too late.

Dr. Arnold shoved his way through the gawking onlookers. There, slumped on the floor, was James Jones Stark. The doctor quickly examined Stark's gaping wound, and checked the man's pulse.

"He's dead," said the doctor.

He looked up at his friend, Dr. Minis. Disheveled and crazed, Minis struggled against Wayne and Spalding. At one point, the doctor threatened to fire into the crowd, somehow forgetting that he had yet to reload.

"My carriage is across Bay at the Exchange," said Dr. Arnold. "Tell the driver to take him to my office. I'll have the sheriff meet us there...."

January 1833

The bailiff peered into the room and motioned toward counsel.

"Well, gentlemen," said Mr. Charlton, pocketing his watch. "It appears the jury has made up their minds."

The defense team settled into the courtroom and waited for the arrival of Judge Dougherty. Dr. Minis leaned over to Mr. Charlton.

"I thought a short deliberation was only good news for the prosecution," he whispered.

"We shall see."

The bailiff held the chambers door for Judge Dougherty. His arrival prompted those gathered in the courtroom to rise to their feet in anticipation of the bailiff's request.

"All rise! Chatham County Court is now in session. The honorable Charles Dougherty presiding."

The judge smoothed his robes and settled into his chair.

"Please be seated," said the judge, sifting through various documents.

"I understand you have reached a verdict. Will you please hand the bailiff your decision?"

The foreman stood and handed a slip of paper to the bailiff, who brought it over to Judge Dougherty. The judge unfolded the parchment and read the decision to himself. He jotted down a few notes, and then looked to the jury.

"Please read your decision to the court, Mr. Foreman."

"In the matter of the State vs. Dr. Philip Minis, on the charge of murder, we, the jury, find the defendant...."

Minis bowed his head, and drew in a deep breath. He was prepared for the worst.

"Not guilty."

Dr. Minis slumped into his chair. It was finally over.

No one knows what Stark was reaching for on that August day. No weapon was found on his person. The Anti-dueling Association did send letters encouraging arbitration; though Mr. Spalding never received his letter before he and Dr. Minis left for the City Hotel. James Stark did receive his, and was considering his reply when he decided to go to the City Hotel. After his acquittal, Dr. Minis would go on to serve his country as a surgeon in the U.S. Army, would father seven children, and would serve on several benevolent committees here in Savannah. Despite growing opposition to "affairs of honor" and the link to intemperance, dueling would continue in Savannah until 1877, when two lawyers met to argue not with words in court, but with pistols at dusk. Both survived, having missed their marks, and went on to be successful leaders.

The rumor that Stark haunts the City Hotel (now Moon River Brewery) persists to this very day. There are Savannahians who swear that, during the extensive renovations necessary to convert the hotel to the Hostess City's only brewery, they saw shadowy figures carry a man through the doorway — and vanish into thin air.

A Shipbuilder and His Lady

Summer, 1864

He called her, "Lady...."

In tender moments, he would cradle her face in his calloused hands and say, "Lady, a man could navigate the darkest seas by the stars in your eyes."

Lady might have laughed outright at such a line, but she knew Henry as a frugal man who saved his words, spending them only when necessary. Sometimes, he saw fit to bellow that term of endearment in frustration, perhaps when she took too long to dress.

"Lady!"

"It wouldn't do for me to be seen out of sorts," she'd say, pinning up her hair.

"It's two in the morning," he'd growl, through teeth clenched tight on his meerschaum.

"Precisely."

Henry rolled his eyes. Lady noticed this in the reflection of her mirror and thought better of making comment on his gesture. Instead, she put him to work.

"Do be a dear and help me cinch my corset," she said. "And please be careful. I know you're anxious to go."

"Not anxious." He tugged firmly on the drawstrings.

"Eager," she grunted.

Henry strode down Price Street, to the river. All the way, Lady kept reminding him to slow down; that a gentleman belonged at the lady's side.

"But we're missing it!" he said, pouting.

Lady pulled him close to her and craned her neck to kiss his bearded cheek. Henry sighed. Whatever it was he wanted to show her wasn't nearly as important as sharing it with her....

"Won't be long before she slips her cradle," said Henry. He wrapped his heavy hands around her cinched waist and lifted Lady up and over the rail.

"Mind your step. I've got block and tackle and all manner of things strewn about."

"She's beautiful," said Lady. "But not much different than when you last showed me."

"True," he said, "but this schooner isn't why I brought you here."

Henry took Lady by hand. They navigated their way through coils of rope and stacks of lumber until they reached the quarterdeck.

"Lady's first." Henry smirked.

"I think, sir, that you just wish to peek at my finery," said Lady, carefully ascending the steep and narrow steps.

The quarterdeck was piled with folds of canvas – sails for the schooner. As Lady looked around for a place to sit, Henry bounded on to the deck and threw himself into the piles of heavy cloth.

Henry smiled, patting a place beside him.

"Henry Willink!" said Lady, her face turning deep crimson. "If you think I came all the way down here to…."

"Lady!" Henry pointed skyward.

Lady looked to the night sky. She had never seen anything like this. A streak of light! Then another! And another!

"I've been waiting for this all year," said Henry. "Now, will you please join me?"

Lady gingerly pawed her way to her husband, unable to take her eyes off the fantastic spectacle. Nestled in his arms, the two gazed at the heavens as streaks of light filled the sky.

The cackle of crows announced the dawn.

Caw! Caw!

Lady stirred.

Caw! Caw! Caw!

She sat bolt upright. Cackling crows cocked their heads.

Lady looked around for Henry. She could hear her husband arguing with someone below deck. She crept toward the fo'c'sle and pressed her ear against the bulkhead.

"You might as well have an albatross around your neck!"

"Miller!"

"Henry! We're behind schedule! And you know how important this contract is!"

"I've been working on this ship in my own time! If we're behind schedule, it's because of the blockade, not because I choose to spend time with my wife.

"She is welcome aboard any time, on this, or any other ship of mine!"

The hatch crashed open. Lady hid herself behind a stack of lumber and watched the murder of crows take flight from the jib boom.

Miller stormed off the schooner.

Henry stepped on to the deck; his shoulders slumped. He turned his gaze toward the quarterdeck, hoping to find Lady, yet hoping to find her gone. Behind him, he heard her sniffle.

"How much did you hear?" he said without turning around.

"Enough," she replied, gently dabbing her eyes.

Lady stood up and tried to push hair back into place. "I'll let you get back to work," she said as she passed, not having the heart to look at her husband.

Henry caught her by the arm and pulled her close.

"You know Miller. All business," he said, brushing the hair from her eyes. "And, I don't need him to help me finish this ship."

Lady looked into his eyes.

"She slips the cradle today, and I want you to be aboard for it!"

Henry leaned over the rail and surveyed the workers below. Strong men. Good workers, too – worth every penny Willink & Miller shelled out for them. Henry would have preferred that these men worked on the CSS *Georgia*, but materials for the ironclad were slow in coming ever since the Yanks captured Fort Pulaski. Miller may not have agreed with Henry's "distraction," but both men knew it was best to keep the crew working, even on something as frivolous as the yet-un-christened schooner.

"What are you going to name her?" Lady asked, dressed in her finest. Henry gazed at the light dancing on the Savannah River.

"You know," said Henry, looking over his shoulder. "I hadn't decided."

"But isn't it…."

"Bad luck not to name a ship?" Henry turned around and leaned on the rail.

"So they say," he continued. "But, if I were a superstitious man, I wouldn't have you on my ship at all, now, would I?"

Henry leaned forward and kissed his wife on the forehead.

"Now, don't stand too close to the rail. We're about to launch the ship."

Henry moved to the aft of the schooner and bent over the gunwale, bracing himself on the capstan.

"All hands! On my command, release the chocks!"

The workers below scrambled to get out from under the ship, while others grabbed the ropes that would pull the massive blocks from the greased cradle.

"Ready on the starboard?" Henry barked from the wheel.

"Aye!" the workers replied.

"Ready on the port?"

"Aye!"

"On my mark...."

Henry looked over his shoulder one last time. Lady was beaming with pride.

"PULL!"

With a mighty tug, the great blocks were wrenched from the cribbing, and the schooner slid toward the Savannah River.

"Yeeee-haww!" cried Henry, grinning as the two-master smashed onto the river with a tremendous splash. The crew cheered and applauded as the spray rained down on them.

Lady hadn't expected the ship to hit the water with such force. As she scrambled to keep her balance, her heel caught the edge of a forgotten serving mallet. She stumbled backward, reaching for the mainstay....

"HENRY!"

Lady tumbled over the edge of the gunwale.

"LADY!"

Henry released the wheel and dashed portside. Frantic, he called out to her.

A few yards out, she surfaced. Henry took a few steps back, then sprinted for the rail. He threw himself off the ship and dove into the river.

As the water embraced him, he realized the current was moving fast – too fast!

Lady struggled. Her layered dress suddenly was much too heavy, and she could feel the undercurrent of the river reaching for her, like tendrils from the abyss.

"Henry!" she cried, reaching for him as the river, desperate to return to the sea, took her under one last time.

"Lady!"

Henry snapped up, breathing hard. His sheets were drenched in sweat. He looked over to the empty place beside him.

Lady.

Henry collapsed onto the bed. He buried his face in her pillow, hoping for just the slightest hint of her scent; praying that this was all some phantasm of the mind.

Hours passed….

He gathered himself together. Wearily, he pulled his trousers over his nightshirt, not caring. After all, it *was* two in the morning. He shoved his feet into his heavy boots, slapped a cap on his head and stepped out into the night.

Henry shuffled down Price Street, toward the river. Overhead, stars streaked across the sky unnoticed. He wished Lady were there. He missed the way she would hold his arm as they walked, or how she would ask him to slow down, just a little, so they could walk together.

As he passed the workers' quarters on State Street, he felt something....

He glanced over his shoulder to see Ol' Jeb leaning out the window. Henry might have chided Ol' Jeb for being up so late, but that was before Lady was called home to Glory. Feeling self-conscious from the look of worry on Jeb's weathered face, Henry merely nodded his head. Ol' Jeb softened his expression ever so slightly, and returned the gesture as if to say, "Don't you worry, Marse Henry."

He shuffled along the cobblestones on River Street; the echo sounded like a breathless whisper calling his name.

H-h-h-enry-y-y-y-y-y....

Henry shivered. He closed his eyes.

"Easy, Henry," he said to himself, resuming his walk.

H-h-h-enry-y-y-y-y-y....

He chided himself for letting his tired mind get the best of him, and picked up his pace. The ship, now just a few yards away, might as well have been docked across the ocean. Out of the corner of his eye, he thought he saw someone standing on deck....

"A trick of the light," he said, stomping up the gangplank.

A wave of nausea hit him as he stepped on to the deck of the schooner.

Slowly, he shuffled to the quarterdeck, trying desperately to imagine their last night together. As he timidly climbed the narrow steps to the deck, he remembered how she flirted with him, ever so subtly, as a lady would do. Shaking, he raised his head and stared blankly at the deck once piled with billowing canvas. For a moment, they were still cuddling there, watching stars above that still went unnoticed.

He crawled to the place where they laid together. He pulled off his coat, though the air was cool and damp, and clutched it to his chest as if he were still holding his wife. Sobbing, his face buried deep in his jacket, Henry drifted off to sleep.

Shouting workers and clanging metal announced the dawn. Henry slowly sat up and shielded his eyes from the morning light.

"Henry!"

Henry jumped at the sound of Miller's booming voice.

"Henry, we need you!" said Miller.

Henry stared into nothing.

"The *Georgia* is leaking like a sieve, and the motor isn't powerful enough to move her!" Miller leaned into Henry's face. "Do you hear me? She's useless!

"Henry! Damn it, man!"

Miller stomped over to the fo'c'sle and leaned over the rail.

"Rig up the towing cables!" he bellowed. "We'll drag her out to Fort Jackson and use her as a gun platform if we have to!"

Miller strode off the ship. Henry barely noticed.

Eventually, Henry rolled up his sleeves and gathered up supplies: a bucket of blue paint, a brush, and a length of rope. He tied two half hitches around the bucket's handle and lowered it over the side, near the bowsprit. Then, as makeshift scaffolding, he tossed the Jacob's ladder over. He shoved the paintbrush in his waistband and climbed over the side.

Henry settled on to the ladder rung and stared at the strakes. As he dipped the brush into the bucket, he allowed himself a wistful smile. Carefully, he dragged the brush gently down the strakes. In clean, even strokes, he began to name the ship.

As he pulled the last stroke, he paused to admire his work....

LADY

Henry felt a strange calm wash over him. He glanced up at the rail.

"Lady?"

There she stood, smiling at her husband, reaching for him.

"Lady!" Henry scrambled to reach her, but his bootstrap caught on the ladder. Into the Savannah River he fell. As the current began pulling him down river, Henry looked back at the schooner. Lady shimmered into nothingness.

Henry smiled, and waited for the currents to take him to his wife....

Henry would have to wait to join his wife. Pulled from the water, he would go on to build a total of four ships for the Confederacy: the ironclads Georgia, Savannah, *and* Milledgeville, *and the wooden gunboat,* CSS Macon.

Years later, just before his cottage was moved from Price and Oglethorpe to East Saint Julian Street, residents claimed they heard the slamming of a door and heavy footsteps walking toward the river. Most believed it was just Henry, on his way to finish his work.

Come to Scratch

The Confederates have gone out of this war, with the proud, secret, deathless, dangerous consciousness that they are THE BETTER MEN.

E.A. Pollard, 1865

December 1864

Every time Red Pickrin passed the Mercer House, he wanted to spit. The house promised to be a real jewel in Savannah's crown, and he was proud to have had a hand in building it. But the cold shadow of civil war blanketed the land, taking with it the best and brightest, among them, General Hugh Mercer. While the good General was off fighting for Southern honor and states' rights, his brick Italianate home would remain unfinished and boarded up — along with any hope of Red finishing his apprenticeship as a mason.

Five years, he thought. *Five damn long years.*

When the call to arms went out to all able-bodied Southern men, Red was among the first to stand in the back of the line. Oh, he wanted to fight, all right, but Red always had a way of showing up a little too late. It was his nature. He would have lost the bricklaying job at the Mercer house if a friend of a friend hadn't talked his dear sweet mother into snatchin' him up by the ear and draggin' him to the work site at Monterey Square, just north of Forsyth Park. (Some might have said that Red was a bit of a mama's boy — except for his mama, that is.)

Still, Red made his way to the recruiting station and found the square mobbed with recruits, young and old — all eager to live and die for Dixie. By the time he got anywhere near the front of the line, they were turning folks away. Still, Red made a point of talking loud to the sergeant — if for no other reason than to show those around him that he gave a damn. The sergeant politely took his information and promised to contact him should the need arise.

Sometime during 1862, Mrs. Pickrin heard a knock at the door. A Confederate sergeant came a-callin' for young Red and said the Confederacy was in dire need of his services. Having lost a husband and her oldest son to the Dreadful Pestilence some eight years earlier, she wasn't about to lose her youngest due to the Recent Unpleasantness. Oh no. That would never do. So, while Red was out taking up odd jobs and lending a hand where he could, she feigned an illness, or two. She swore she was suffering from a relapse of Yellow Fever (until Red found the emetics under her bed). Then, she claimed she had a wasting disease (until the physician said she was healthy as a horse, which Mrs. Pickrin took as an insult to her "womanly figure" and took to beating the doctor about the head and shoulders). In the end, Red decided that it was best for him to stay home and care for his mama, lest she die of a broken heart.

Now, having seen what the Union had done to his beloved Savannah, he'd've given his right arm for the chance to shoot a couple of Yanks. Like a plague of locusts, they descended upon his city, tearing up everything in their path. By some accounts, Sherman's men had already removed a couple of thousand cartloads of manure — and they still had a ways to go. (Some, like Mrs. Pickrin, thought that the Union soldiers themselves ought to be piled high on those carts of manure as they were wheeled out of the city proper.)

And so, as was his habit, Red trudged by the Mercer House and found a whole new reason to spit fire: those damned Yanks were tearing the boards off the windows and were using them to construct lean-tos against the Pulaski Monument!

"Hell, no!" spat Red, rolling up his sleeves. He looked for the man with the most stripes on his sleeve and trudged on over, ready to take on the whole damned Union Army, if he had to.

Private Beechnut hadn't been in the Union Army for much longer than the time it had taken him to march through boot camp. The way he saw it, a stint in the military was a good way to get out of being an ironworker. Better still, it was a great way to get out of Cleveland. Now here he was, serving in the Union Army under that great general, William Tecumseh Sherman — and at the end of his March to the Sea at that. Beechnut had hoped to record all that he had seen, but the army never saw fit to teach him to read or write. So, he stumbled along, asking others to write his letters for him. It was a leap of faith, since he still had a very limited understanding of the written word. For all he knew, his "buddies" could have been telling tall tales about his exploits. (In a way, he kind of hoped they would. After all, Beechnut had a girl to impress back home. No, they weren't engaged, nor were they even courting, but he wanted to impress her just the same.)

Beechnut and his bunkmate, Corporal Newbury, wedged their bayonets into the space between the brick and the boards and wrenched the planks off the windows.

"I hear this is the home of a Confederate General!" said Beechnut.

"Yep," said Newbury. "Hugh Mercer. Don't know much about him, though."

"Me, neither," said Beechnut. "But I still don't get why we can't all just bunk in the house itself."

"Unit cohesiveness," said Newbury.

"Unit what?" The men cradled the planks under their arms and stepped back from the house.

"It means we all live under the same rules and conditions." An ammunition caisson rumbled by. Newbury raised a free hand to wave at the riders as they passed.

"It wouldn't do if we were all cozy in this brick home while our comrades at arms slept under the stars, now would it?"

"Guess not," said Beechnut.

"Besides," said Newbury, "we'll need the wood floors for firewood."

Suddenly, Beechnut crashed into the back of Newbury.

"Dammit, Beechnut!"

"It wasn't me!" said Beechnut. "I was shoved!"

The two men looked over their shoulder to find Red Pickrin, mad as a Kentucky gamecock.

Beechnut sprang to his feet and shoved Pickrin hard. Pickrin stumbled back.

"What the hell do you think you're doing, cracker!"

Pickrin stood nose to nose with Beechnut. "Y'all ain't got no business tearin' up this house! Now take these boards an' put 'em back where you found 'em!"

Newbury placed a firm hand on Beechnut's shoulder. Beechnut backed away from the men.

"You know we can't do that, sir," said Newbury. His was a smile that seemed warm at first blush, but left a man cold. "We need to make camp."

"I could give a rat's ass," Red snarled. "Y'all come wanderin' into town like you own the place — which you don't — and y'all promised to take care of our people and our property — which you ain't — "

Newbury flashed that unnerving smile like he was running for office. "Sir, I understand your — "

"You understand nothin'." Red punctuated his remark with a hock and spit. He looked around and found a crowd of bluecoats gathering, every one of them a little more than eager to beat the tar out of the hotheaded Johnny Reb.

"Look around you, son," said the corporal, his smile fading into an icy, clenched-jaw stare. "You can't win this fight."

"Not today," said Red. He shoved his way past Newbury and Beechnut.

Red stomped up the stairs of their modest townhouse at Mary Marshall Row. He fumbled with the keys, stepped in and slammed the door.

"Red Pickrin!" came the sound of his mother's voice. "You know better than to slam the door when you walk in!"

Red said nothing. He knew anything out of his mouth would set her off even more, and apologizing for something he felt justified in doing, well, that wasn't about to happen. Instead, he quietly blew out a breath and made his way upstairs to the master bedroom. About half way up, he heard his mother call again.

"Red, baby."

Her voice just gets on my nerves.

"Bring Mama some sweet tea before you come up."

Red sighed and walked back downstairs, hoping to find some already made up. When he got to the pantry, he cursed.

Of course, there ain't no sweet tea.

He opened a canister, then another, and another.

Ain't got no tea. No sugar. That's just great.

He plodded to the bottom of the stairs, leaned on the banister and called up to his mother.

"Mama," he called. "Ain't no sweet tea."

"What?!?"

Red took a breath. He just knew what was coming.

"Ain't got no sweet tea, Mama."

Mrs. Pickrin shifted her great weight in her bed. She heard Red quite clearly — she had excellent hearing — but hated being barked at. She did, after all, carry the little whelp in her belly for nearly a year.

"Baby, you know I can't hear all that well. Not since the fever." She stretched out her thick arm and gazed at her tiny little nails, as if they were diamonds in the rough. "Now come on up and talk to me like a gentleman."

Red trudged up the stairs. Slowly, he rounded the banister. Then, he shuffled to the door of his mother's room. He leaned in the doorway and dropped his head.

"Ain't no sweet tea, Mama."

"No sweet tea? Go make your mama some sweet tea, baby."

"Can't, Mama." Red stared at the wall.

Mrs. Pickrin supported herself on her elbows.

"Well, why not?" Mrs. Pickrin had a way of finishing most of her sentences with jaw-agape. Sometimes, depending on the inflection, her jowls would wobble for about a second after she pronounced the last syllable.

"We got no sugar. No tea. Can't make your sweet tea without them, now can I?" Oh, he was fighting hard to be civil.

"Did you have a bad day baby? Just go on down to market an' get what we need."

"Can't."

"Now you're jus' bein' difficult."

"Mama," he could feel his temples throb. "Maybe it's been a while since you went to market yourself — and I know you're not feeling well — but things are… different."

Mrs. Pickrin shoved herself upright.

"In my drawer is some money — "

Red ripped open the drawer and seized a handful of Confederate dollars.

"This money?" He slammed the drawer shut.

"This?!" Red stalked over to the bed and fluttered the bills in her face. Mrs. Pickrin grabbed the covers and drew them up to hide.

"This money was worthless — WORTHLESS — before them Yanks rolled into town. How much do you think it is worth now? Hmmm?! *Before* they showed up, you'd have to tote a lifesavings in a market basket. You know what that got you, Mama? A half-a-sack of grits — maybe! And then, you'd have to leave the basket as payment!

"Now we need greenbacks — and lots of them — and we ain't got no way to get 'em!"

Mrs. Pickrin tried hard to still her quivering lip. Red stomped over to the dresser and yarded open drawer after drawer.

"Any greenbacks hiding in here? No. Of course not! Because you never leave this room!"

Red heard a soft sniffle come from under the covers. He dropped his head and quietly closed the last drawer.

"I'm sorry, Mama." He couldn't bear to look at her. He knew he wouldn't be able to say what he wanted to say if he did. Instead, he traced small circles in the dust on the dresser.

"It's just that, well, I missed my chance... and now, it's too late to do anything about it."

Red turned toward the door. He knew he should rush right over and comfort his mother, but he just couldn't break through that wall that had been building inside him ever since the recruiting sergeant turned him away. He always wondered why he was never called to service....

"I'll get your sweet tea, Mama." Red shuffled out the door. As he started down the stairs, he whispered, "Somehow."

He knew that getting tea, let alone sugar, would be a Sisyphean task. The Yanks were the only ones in town with any money to spend — and none of it went back to rebuilding the crippled economy. Sure, Billy Yank was all too happy to throw money after lame horses on some makeshift racetrack. He was even happier to take advantage of starving Confederate widows, assuaging his guilt by leaving a few greenbacks on her bedside table. Then, as he threw more money at the bartenders, he would sully her good name by bragging about his conquest.

Red glanced up to see a couple of young ladies cross the street expressly to avoid walking under the Union flag. How he admired their courage. Even in their threadbare dresses, these ladies carried themselves with both prevenient grace and steel-jawed courage. Such resolve prompted Sherman himself to say that Savannah women were "the toughest set" he ever knew. One moment, the Confederate wives were selling sweetbread to the bluecoats, and the next, these same women would turn their backs on those same soldiers as they passed in muster.

Sherman was right, he thought. *The women of Savannah would have kept this war going long after the men had given up.*

Red crossed Drayton Street at Bay Lane. He knew the barkeep, Johnny Ray, and hoped that he might know of anyone who was hiring. As he opened the door, Newbury and Beechnut staggered out. He thought about jumping them in the lane, but knew that would be suicide.

Keep it holstered, he told himself. Red breathed a sigh of relief when the men passed without recognizing him. Oh, he was ready to throw down, all right, but now wasn't the time or the place.

He stepped into the room. The place was crawling with bluecoats, two or three deep at the bar. He shook his head. He'd never get Johnny Ray's attention at this rate, and he just couldn't bear the thought of jumping behind the bar to serve these sons-a-bitches, even if it meant sweet tea for his mama. But as Red turned to leave, a broadsheet tacked to the doorpost caught his eye. The header read: *Last Man Standing*. Red snatched the sheet off the wall and bolted out the door. He found himself a way to get some money — and beat some Yankee ass!

Red loved to scrap. Granted, sometimes it was in the defense of his mother's good name (often due to his mother's public preening and doting), but Red had to thank his mama, even for that. He knew that he could hold his own if it came to blows, and he was glad. It would soon pay off, hopefully big!

The Yanks, in their boredom, started holding boxing matches in the backrooms of barrooms, especially behind the pub where Johnny Ray worked. Granted, you had to enter from the alley, but that worked just fine. Those that wanted to bet on the fight could; those that just wanted to put away the day wouldn't be bothered by the rowdy crowd.

Johnny Ray was a sharp guy. He took on the responsibility of taking bets, keeping the odds, posting the rankings, and he did a fine job of it — especially for a man who had to learn it all on the fly. That Johnny Ray was the one pairing up the fighters was good news for Red. If all went according to his plan (and if Johnny Ray agreed), Red would only have to fight Yankees, and he had one in mind — that private he saw ripping boards off the Mercer House. There was no rhyme or reason for his hatred of the young man. After all, they were about the same age and might have even been good friends in nobler times, but like two dogs who can't stand each other's scent, he just wanted to tear into that kid like nobody's business.

Red waited around until Johnny Ray was closing up, and then invited himself in for a drink. Johnny Ray listened to Red's plan, and waited until he said what he had to say.

"Sorry, Red," said Johnny Ray. "It doesn't work that way."

"Why the hell not?"

Johnny Ray leaned on the bar. "Because the Yanks have this bruiser that's been bustin' jaws all week.

Some ringer they brought in from Massachusetts. I hear he's down here, settin' things up for a colored regiment."

"Is he a Negro?"

"Naw, man. Some mick from Beantown. He'll clean your clock, son. I seen it."

"Then put me in first, so I can get it over with."

Not long after donning the gray, Johnny Ray Banks found himself on the mist-shrouded battlefield of Chickamauga Creek. Shrapnel from an exploding mortar took his left eye and shattered his eardrum. The blast knocked him so cold that, in the fog of war, his comrades had all but left him for dead. Needless to say, Johnny never talked much about the war, and folks knew better than to ask. In a strange way, the bluecoats that now frequented his pub did so because they wanted to lay eyes on a gray-back who survived that bloody battle. Johnny Ray didn't care, as long as they kept tipping.

Yep, Johnny Ray had seen a lot of things in his thirty-five years, so when he looked into Red's eyes, he witnessed the fire of a young man who had already forged his decision.

"You're in," said Johnny Ray. And with that, he scratched the name of some Yankee private named Beechnut off the list, and wrote: *R. Pickrin.*

Friday night came fast. Red made up some excuse about picking up a last minute delivery job for Johnny Ray. He certainly didn't want his mother to know about his plan for winning five hundred greenbacks — the prize for defeating the Yankee Bruiser, as he was now called. She would worry herself sick.

Despite the curfew, the back room to the pub was packed with rowdies and regulars. A handful of carpetbaggers intending to pass through Savannah on the way to Charleston found themselves with little to do, since so many pubs and restaurants had closed up earlier than expected. They placed the highest bets of all — and always on the odds-on favorite.

"Gentlemen, please!" said Johnny Ray, holding up his hands. "Y'all just settle down, now."

A hush fell over the room.

"Alright, then. If you hadn't placed your bet on the first fight, you flat outta luck. Time has done run out."

A murmur rolled through the room as bluecoats clutched their tickets.

"Now, our champ-een has been cleaning the clocks of young bucks all week."

The crowd stomped their feet and cheered. Johnny Ray held his hands up, waving them down a bit.

"Hopefully tonight, he won't be quite so bored."

Bluecoats guffawed and snickered.

"This is a *Last Man Standing* bout," said Johnny Ray, thrusting a finger at the elimination brackets tacked to the wall. "Y'all know what that means. The longer our champ stays in the ring, the larger the pot grows."

The men hooted and cheered.

"If he becomes the last man standing, he stands to win half of the prize money — which I suspect will go a long way to nurse his wounds!"

A raucous laughter filled the room. With a gleam in his eye, Johnny Ray continued.

"I know it's unlikely, but if a challenger should best our champ — "

The men in blue booed and jeered. Johnny Ray raised his voice to shout above the noise.

"If a challenger should defeat our champ, he'll take home five-hundred greenbacks and come on back next week to become the Last Man Standing!"

The Yanks stomped their feet and threw playful jabs at each other. Johnny kept right on talking.

"Now, if you still don't know about Broughton's Rules, I ain't gonna explain 'em now, except to say that the round doesn't end until one of 'em gets knocked on his ass, and the fight doesn't end until one of 'em is slapped so silly he can't come to scratch. Could take five minutes. Could last all night.

"So, without further delay, let me call these boys in here."

Private Beechnut slid out of his jacket and was already receiving pats on the back from Newbury and the boys.

"Our first fighter is a local boy, from right here in Savannah."

Beechnut and Newbury exchanged awkward glances.

"Weighing in at a very lean 170 pounds, R-r-r-r-ed Pickrin-n-n-n-n!"

As the crowd jeered, Red bounced his way passed the stunned Beechnut and Newbury. He stepped in the ring and gave a quick nod and a wink to Beechnut. He then thumped his chest with his fists and pointed at Newbury. Johnny Ray glanced around and waited for the crowd to settle. With a flourish, he raised his hands high.

"And now, all the way from Boston, Massachusetts...."

The room exploded with stomping feet and warlike cries.

"Tipping the scales at a whopping 210 pounds...."

The Bruiser shrugged out of his jacket — and he had to work at it. Johnny Ray motioned toward the big Irishman.

"The Yankee-e-e-e Bruiser-r-r...."

The big Irishman threw a couple of lighting fast jabs to the delight of the crowd and danced into the makeshift ring.

"Kerr-r-r-r-y Garr-r-r-rett!!!!"

The thunderous applause erupting from the Yanks never bothered Red, nor did it bother him that the Bruiser was a head taller. Red had all the focus and tenacity of a foxhound on a rabbit. The intensity of his stare and the wild look in his eyes made the Bruiser shift his gaze, if only for a split second.

"If you're gonna fight under my roof," said Johnny Ray, "then you're gonna fight by the rules. Don't hit a man when he's down. Don't wrestle or tackle. Don't fight like a girl and pull hair or nothin'. Round ends when one a'y'all takes a knee or gets knocked down, and if ya can't come to this line right here after half-a-minute, that's all she wrote. Got it?"

The men nodded. Red spit on the floor.

"Now, I'm gonna get on out the way," Johnny Ray said. "When I do, y'all start fightin'."

Before Johnny Ray could slip out of the make-shift ring, Red threw a vicious right cross, knocking the Bruiser to the floor. The men jeered and cussed.

"Get up!" said the prancing Red. "I'm'o whoop yer ass, boy!"

The Bruiser brushed his lip with the back of his hand. Red clenched his fists. He had waited for this moment for too long. Four years of pulling his punches and holding his tongue, all for the sake of Southern decorum and mother's modesty, was directed at the burly brute that, in Red's mind, had become the very symbol of Northern Oppression. Someone was going to fall tonight, and Red was going to make damn sure it wasn't him.

"Get up!"

The Bruiser stood and brought his fists up. He stepped for the line. The moment he came to scratch, Red threw the same right cross. The Bruiser ducked and smashed Red in the gut. He doubled over. The Yank followed with a brutal uppercut, sending Red into the crowd. The bluecoats shoved Red back at the Bruiser, who launched a heavy-handed cross. Red bobbed and landed a sharp hook to the Yank's ribs. The Bruiser wheeled around and clumsily threw a left. Red ducked and popped him in the ribs again, then threw a right hook at the Yank's head. Their arms locked, and the men found themselves in a tight clinch.

"Not bad, kid," the Bruiser growled. "You got a lot of heart!"

Red shoved the Bruiser off, sending him into the crowd. A couple of men shoved the Bruiser headlong into Red's waiting fists.

Men booed.

Bruiser stumbled back. The gavel fell.

CLACK-CLACK

"I'm alright," said the Bruiser, bouncing to his feet. He glided into the ring, threw a jab, then another, then a quick shot to the gut, followed by a sharp hook to Red's head. Red crumpled to the floor.

Men cheered.

"Kick his cracker ass!"

The gavel fell. Newbury slapped Beechnut across the back and shouted.

"I told you this was gonna be good!"

And so it went, the boxer versus the brawler. Some rounds lasted a few seconds. Some lasted more than twenty minutes.

Worn and weary, his eye cut and swollen, the Bruiser stumbled into Red who threw a sharp jab at the Bruiser's wounded eye. The Bruiser stumbled back, but was pursued relentlessly by Red, who pummeled him, one sharp, hard blow after another.

The Bruiser collapsed at Newbury's feet. The corporal took a knee and tried to rouse the big Yank.

"Kerry!" said Newbury. "Get up, you chicken-shit Mick!"

Johnny Ray banged the gavel.

CLACK-CLACK-CLACK

Newbury turned ashen. Murmurs echoed throughout the room. Bluecoats cussed and tore up their tickets. Locals laughed. Red staggered a bit, and then dragged a sweaty forearm across his bloody mouth.

"He killed him!" shouted Newbury. He sprang to his feet and thrust a finger at the now-sluggish Red. "That cracker killed him!"

Union troops pounced on Red like a pack of rabid dogs. Too weak to fight back, all he could do was take the beating: hard kicks to the ribs, sharp punches to the face and head. Red found himself smiling. He couldn't help himself. He just knew that sweet tea would taste so good.

"That son of a bitch!" cried a stocky sergeant. "I'll take that smile right off his face!"

The soldier raised his leg high and drove the arch of his riding boot onto Red's neck.

CRACK!

An eerie hush fell over the room. The men looked at one another with fear in their eyes. Before anyone knew what had really happened, they heard a quiet murmur from the corner of the room. The Bruiser stirred and groaned.

The Yanks exchanged nervous glances as Johnny Ray forced his way through the crowd.

Johnny felt a wave of nausea roll over him when he saw Red's lifeless body. He slumped to the floor and gathered Red in his arms. He watched helplessly as Red's head lolled to one side, like that of a rag doll. Then, with a soldier's resolve, Johnny Ray Banks carefully laid Red down and draped the young man's coat over his battered face. He dropped his head just long enough to catch his breath.

"Who did this?" Johnny asked. He scanned the room. Carpetbaggers were slinking out the back as if nothing had happened. Johnny looked up to see Corporal Newbury patting a sergeant on the shoulder.

"Got somethin' to tell me, corporal?" he said. He seized Newbury's arm and wheeled him around. Johnny Ray was met with that blasted smile.

"Your friend put up one hell of a fight," said Newbury. "Surprised us all."

"You kill him?" Johnny Ray stood nose-to-nose with Newbury. "Or was it that ape of a sergeant?"

Without flinching, Newbury called out.

"Sergeant Grimes. Did you break this man's neck?"

Grimes folded his arms.

"He died in the fight, corporal," sneered Grimes. Newbury smirked.

"Private Beechnut."

The young private straightened up.

"Yes, sir?"

"Who killed this man?"

Beechnut lowered his eyes. He found himself suddenly preoccupied by the leather band of his kepi.

"I can't hear you, private!"

Beechnut snapped up.

"He died in the fight, corporal!"

Newbury smiled. How he loved unit cohesion.

"I may be wrong, Mr. Banks, but if I took roll right here and now, I bet I'd find a room full of Union soldiers who would all say that your friend here died in the fight."

He inched closer to Johnny Ray.

"So, tell me, Mr. Banks," said Newbury, as the bluecoats closed ranks. "Do you think a one-eyed Jack can beat a full house?"

Days had passed, and Mrs. Pickrin still heard no word from her son. Given that Red was the only one to check in on her, Mrs. Pickrin took it upon herself to dress, but one look at the moth-eaten garment and she realized that she could no longer fit into it. She waddled over to a steamer trunk, pulled out some black fabric and her sewing kit, and began stitching herself a new dress. It took her week of hand stitching to finish the dress, and she found herself marveling at the delicate work.

How long has it been? She wondered.

She bathed herself, stepped into her dress, and looked for her shoes. From under the bed, she dragged a pair of dust-covered, ankle-high boots. She braced her great weight on the bed and forced herself up with a grunt. Then, she eased herself onto the worn bed. With a grumble, she dragged her ankle up onto her knee and tried to shoehorn her wide foot into the boot. Now two sizes too small, she knew they'd never fit. She groaned and threw the boot across the room.

"Barefoot it is," she said. "If folks don't like it, that ain't my problem."

Mrs. Pickrin did her hair as best she could, snapped up a black lace bonnet, and dusted off her parasol. She labored down the narrow stairs, stopping along the way.

Lord have mercy.

At the bottom of the stairs, she took a hard look at herself in the mirror.

What happened to you, girl? How could you fall so far?

She could feel her chest and throat tighten. Mrs. Pickrin knew the tears were coming, but she didn't have the time to cry. She had to find her son. It was like a kettle boiling over.

Mrs. Pickrin yarded open the door. She popped her parasol to shield her eyes from the light of day. She shook her head in disgust; unable to remember the last time she had felt the sun on her skin.

Down South Broad she walked, parasol in hand. She could feel the stares from Union troops as they passed, but paid them no never mind. At the Gordon home, she settled onto their front steps to catch her breath. She tried to remember exactly where Johnny's pub was.

Drayton Street? Yes, Drayton Street.

She pulled herself up, popped her parasol, and trudged up Bull Street toward Wright Square. She could hardly recognize it. There, surrounding the monument was a Union shantytown. Mrs. Pickrin shook her head in disgust — especially when she overheard a Union general flatter a private for his ingenuity for using a gilded mirror for the door of his lean-to.

Disgraceful!

Mrs. Pickrin fought the urge to spit. She turned down President Street (to avoid walking under a Union flag) and then shuffled up Drayton, almost all the way to Bay Street.

The sign on the door read: CLOSED.

Oh, hell no!

Mrs. Pickrin gathered her sleeve in her hand and dusted off the small window to the corner door. She peered in. The bar was trashed. In the reflection of the shattered mirror, she saw the fractured image of a man sweeping broken glass.

Johnny Ray couldn't remember much about how that night ended. After he threatened to report the soldiers, they took it upon themselves to dispense a little Yankee justice. After their lawless disorder, Johnny didn't have much left to his name. When he woke, the liquor was looted, the furniture demolished; it was a wonder they didn't just burn the place down. If it weren't for the fact that Johnny was smart enough to hire a runner to stash the cash, he would've lost the earnings from the prizefight. Not that it mattered. He was going to have it delivered to Mrs. Pickrin, to pay for his bothersome conscience.

Blood money, he thought.

Worst of all, he had no idea where the Yanks hid Red's body, and nobody was talking.

BANG-BANG-BANG

Johnny Ray squinted through his one good eye. Silhouetted in the tiny window was the face of a large woman wearing a bonnet. He leaned the broom up against the wall, and then did his best to straighten his disheveled hair. Johnny Ray shuffled over to the door.

"Are you Johnny Ray?" Mrs. Pickrin shouted through the window.

"Who wants to know?"

"Did my boy come to see you?" she said, on tiptoe. "Did Red come to see you?"

Johnny unlatched the door and bowed his head. Without a word, he motioned for Mrs. Pickrin to come in.

"Watch your feet, ma'am," he said. "I ain't quite done sweepin' up. Them bluecoats left quite a mess."

Johnny Ray reached in a satchel and pulled out a thick, brown paper envelope. He set it on the bar.

"I'd offer you a seat, Mrs. Pickrin, but the Yanks did a good job of making my bar standing room only."

"It's okay," she replied. "I don't feel much like sitting," With a quick tug, she yarded off her bonnet. Then, she set her parasol on the bar.

Johnny Ray walked down the bar, sliding the envelope along with him. He couldn't bear to tell her that these were earnings from the fight that killed her son.

"Red wanted me to give you this," said Johnny. "He had been saving up for some time, doing odd jobs for me now and then."

Mrs. Pickrin looked up in wonder.

"There's more'n fifteen hundred greenbacks in there."

"But why did he ask you to hold it."

"You know Red," said Johnny, forcing a smile. "He told me that if I didn't hold on to it, he was gonna spend it all on his mama."

Mrs. Pickrin's lip quivered.

Don't cry in front of strangers, she told herself. *It's not ladylike.*

Johnny Ray looked at his splintered reflection in the shattered mirror, and then looked at his hands.

"Mrs. Pickrin," said Johnny. "I'm awful sorry about Red. I don't know what happened to him, or where he is, but you should know that he got into it with some bluecoats — got into it real bad."

Mrs. Pickrin turned stark white. A shiver ran through Johnny like the cold wind of a Nor'easter. He moved closer to Mrs. Pickrin.

"Oh, no," said Johnny Ray, taking her hand. "He wasn't doing anything that would ruin your good name. Not Red. In fact, I hear tell that he was defending your honor."

Mrs. Pickrin looked up at Johnny Ray. She noticed Red's name scribbled on the elimination chart tacked to the post, just over Johnny's shoulder.

"So he was fighting for the cause?"

Johnny nodded.

Mrs. Pickrin gathered her belongings. She tucked the brown paper envelope under her arm and padded toward the door. Then, she placed a hand on the doorknob. She lowered her eyes. She sighed.

"I wouldn't have it any other way."

When Churchill's Pub was located at 9 Drayton Street (it now sits on Bay, next to Moon River Brewery), some of the employees and more than a few customers claim to have heard the sounds of a boxing match emanating from the dining room in the back of the restaurant. Stories like this abound. According to local legend, the broken body of a brawler was unearthed during renovations in the 1920s. Rumor has it the coroner had indicated the man died when his neck was broken. (Other ver-

sions of this story tell of a mob lynching that took place in the pub, but this is apocryphal, at best. Stringing a man up without benefit of a pre-determined drop won't break his neck, but will result in a slow and agonizing strangulation. The scenario depicted in this story is far more plausible.)

Gracie

Spring 1889

Cries rang out from the grand ballroom of the Pulaski Hotel as the band struck up a lively reel. Dozens of men and women in all their finery dashed to the dance floor, eager to kick up their heels to *De Boatmen's Dance*. Little Gracie Watson was no exception. She excused herself from her mother's company and stomped on over to her father (who seemed a little too interested in the grown-ups) and tugged on his waistcoat. Mr. Watson and his guests turned their attention to the source of his distraction.

"Well," said a grinning naval captain. "It seems that a certain young lady desires your company."

The men chuckled. Gracie tried hard not to roll her eyes. That would have been "un-lady like," or so she had been told.

"Best not keep her waiting," said the captain.

Mr. Watson excused himself from the group and took his daughter by the hand. When they got to the center of the floor, he whisked her up in his arms.

"Thank you for saving me," said Mr. Watson. He kissed Gracie on the cheek. She clumsily kissed him back.

Gracie looked around the dance floor. All of the other men and women were spinning around, laughing. Occasionally, they would lock arms with one another, and even change dance partners.

"Poppa, aren't we supposed to be changing hands, like the others?"

"Yes," he said, beaming. "But I want you all to myself!" Suddenly, he wheeled her around the room with fanciful sidesteps to the delight of some four hundred men and women.

Frances Watson clapped her hands to the rhythm of the music. Her eyes sparkled as she watched father and daughter wheel around the dance floor.

"She's a beautiful little girl."

Mrs. Watson turned to the sound of the voice. She smiled and curtsied at the gentleman.

"Mr. Lester, Your Honor," she said, fluttering her lacey fan. "My husband tells me you are running for Congress."

"And he would be right," said Mr. Lester. "First district."

"We wish you luck, Mr. Mayor," she said.

"That's most kind of you," he replied. "But I simply wanted to pay you a compliment before I turn in. This has been a splendid party. Brilliant."

"Why thank you, Your Honor." Mrs. Watson feigned her modesty, as she thought a lady should. Still, she knew full well that she and Mr. Watson would be all but invisible were it not for such extravagant galas. Savannah certainly had its eccentricities, and this was one of them.

"We try very hard," she said. She noticed the Mayor's glass was empty, and waved a servant over to them.

"We're happy to have you," said the Mayor. The young lady strode over and offered her empty serving tray to the mayor.

"You and your husband make us worthy of the moniker, Hostess City," said Mr. Lester. He set his empty glass on the tray and nodded to the young lady. "Well, I should say that honor falls to your lovely daughter."

Applause filled the room as the band closed out *De Boatmen's Dance*. Mrs. Watson smiled. She looked across the dance floor and saw her husband and little Gracie laughing. Mr. Watson set Gracie on the floor. She darted over to her mother.

"How old is she?" asked the mayor.

Gracie crashed into her mother's billowing skirts and hugged her around the legs. She looked at Mr. Lester as if he were some sort of strange creature. Then, she promptly tugged on her mother's sleeve. Mrs. Watson crouched, offering an ear to her daughter. She giggled. Mayor Lester cocked his head inquisitively.

"Miss Gracie asked me to remind you that it is not polite to ask a woman her age," said Mrs. Watson, pursing her lips in mock indignation. Gracie tugged on her sleeve yet again, and whispered into her mother's ear once more.

"But Miss Gracie wishes to inform you that she is six." Mrs. Watson beamed.

Mayor Lester eased himself into a crouch.

"It shall be our little secret, my lady."

Gracie buried herself into her mother's skirts.

"Well, it seems Miss Gracie has had a long day," said Mrs. Watson, caressing her daughter's honeyed hair. Mrs. Watson nodded to her husband. He excused himself from his conversation and strode over to his wife and daughter. She whispered in his ear, and Mr. Watson took his daughter by the hand and led her from the dance floor.

It wasn't too long before guests started approaching Mrs. Watson, inquiring as to the whereabouts of the little hostess.

"Where's Gracie?" they would ask. When informed by Mrs. Watson that little Gracie had turned in for the evening, the guests chuckled. Invariably, they would make some comment regarding the lateness of the hour and of how they should excuse themselves, lest they overstay their welcome.

Mr. Watson opened the door to their suite within the opulent Pulaski House. He had to do a bit of juggling, as he had a sleeping child nestled in his arms. He set little Gracie on the bed and slowly, carefully, lovingly changed her out of her fancy dress and into her shift. Then, he gently laid her to rest in her tiny bed, drew the covers, and kissed her goodnight.

As was his habit, Mr. Watson leaned against the door frame and simply watched her sleep. He wondered (as every doting father) whether any man should be so fortunate as he, to have been blessed with such an angel.

Mr. Watson loosened his cravat and unbuttoned his high collar. Then, he slipped out of his waistcoat and draped it over the hand-carved, cedar valet. He stepped out of his shoes and, rather than move to the master bedroom, he decided to sit in the armchair across from Gracie's bed. He just wanted to hear her breathe. There was something comforting about that. No matter what was wrong with the world, he could always count on that special feeling.

A while later, after the guests had gone home for the evening, Mrs. Watson slipped into their suite. She looked for her husband in their bed, but he was not to be found. She tiptoed around the corner to where she knew he would be, and smiled at the sight of her man, though asleep, watching over their daughter.

Rather than wake him, she draped a comforter over him, and then retired for the evening.

Miss Mathilda had been a chambermaid at the Pulaski Hotel for as long as anyone could remember. Certainly, she had been there long before Mr. Watson had taken over as general manager for the hotel. She, like so many others, was quite taken with Gracie. As she was making her way down the stairs, she heard a winsome giggle. She smiled.

"Ooh! I sure hope that's not a ghost!" she said. Mathilda set her clean linens on the end table at the foot of the stairs. "Because I sure am scared of ghosts!"

The giggling continued.

"Sure wish Miss Gracie were here," she said, creeping around the banister. "She'd know what to do!"

Just then, little Gracie jumped out from under the stairs.

"Here I am!" she said, throwing herself at Miss Mathilda. Mathilda wrapped her arms around the child and pulled her close.

Gracie coughed.

"Chile, cover your mouth when you cough," said Mathilda.

Gracie put a tiny hand over her mouth and coughed again.

"You know your mother is looking for you," she said, with a gleam in her eye.

"I know," said Gracie. "I'm not going anywhere."

Again, she coughed.

Mathilda placed the back of her hand on Gracie's forehead. The smile faded. She moved her hand to the child's cheek.

"I think you are coming down with a cold," said Mathilda. She stood and offered Gracie her hand. "Let's get you to bed."

Gracie scooted under the staircase. She folded her arms and pouted.

"Okay, Miss Gracie," said Mathilda, peering under the staircase. "I don't mind leaving you here, but if your mother and father find out I didn't put you to bed when you had a fever, I would lose my job. Then, my husband, ooh! He would get mad and I'd be in serious trouble. Serious trouble."

Mathilda stood up and moved toward the end table and began smoothing out ironed linens.

"But far be it for me to know what's best for Miss Gracie." She felt a tug on her apron strings.

"Okay," said Gracie. "But only because I don't want you to get into trouble."

At first, there was the cough, and perhaps a low fever. As the days passed, Gracie complained of chills. She told her mother her "tummy hurt." Soon, she couldn't keep anything down. When the physician was called in, he grimly told the Watson's that he believed Gracie had pneumonia, and that there was little he or anyone could do but wait, and pray.

Mrs. Watson kept constant vigil over Gracie. Once the sophisticated socialite, Frances had their meals brought to them in the room. Parties were rescheduled, then postponed, and then canceled.

Mr. Watson buried himself in his work — at least until Miss Mathilda told him he ought to spend as much time with his daughter as he could.

"If something happens, I'll find you," she'd say.

Now, Mr. Watson sat by the bed not because it brought him comfort, but because he felt the desperate need to spend every moment with his daughter. The gentle breath that once brought him such peace was now labored and shallow. When she would fall silent, Mr. Watson would snap out of his catnap and rush to her bedside, placing his ear over her mouth, hoping to feel the tickle of her breath in his ear, and greatly relieved, to the point of tears, when he did.

One cheerless morning, on Good Friday, Gracie was called home to Glory. Mr. and Mrs. Watson cradled their little girl for hours.

When Mathilda heard the news, she wept in solitude. Then, she put on a brave face and went about the Watson's suite, preparing it for deep mourning. She began by hanging a black crepe ribbon on the door to their suite. Then, she informed the rest of the staff not to disturb the Watson's under any circumstances. She let herself in the room and drew the curtains. She turned the clocks back, stopping them at the hour of Gracie's passing. She draped black fabric over the mirrors and finally, she helped prepare Gracie's little body for visitation.

Mathilda noticed that Mrs. Watson had not saved a lock of Gracie's hair. Perhaps, because she was from Northern climes, Mrs. Watson was unaware of the custom of braiding or tatting the hair of a loved one into a delicate flower. So, with the Watson's permission, Miss Mathilda snipped a lock of Gracie's hair and began the meticulous process of tatting a delicate daisy from Gracie's honeyed hair.

The weeks wore on without little Gracie, and her absence took its toll. The hotel was no longer a pleasant place to work. With constant reminders of Gracie at every turn, Mr. Watson found his pleasing profession had become little more than a dreary job. It didn't help at the end of the day to come home to a shadowy suite, still dressed in the trappings of deep mourning. Such was the burden of Victorian living.

Mr. Watson sighed as he trudged down the stairs. He paused at the landing, thinking he heard a child giggling.

Gracie?

Gently, he peered over the balustrade, hoping to see other children playing under the stairs where Gracie spent her waking hours. There below sat Mrs Watson, carrying on a conversation with the shadows under the stairs. Crestfallen, Mr. Watson bowed his head. A tear rolled off his nose and plummeted to the floor below.

Mr. Watson absently waved off the waiter. The afternoon had come and gone unnoticed. Now, he and Mrs. Watson sat across the dinner table at the restaurant in the Pulaski House in silence. He wrestled with the idea of confronting Mrs. Watson with her talks with the late little Gracie, but simply could muster no courage to do so, nor could he find the tender words demanded by this delicate situation. Disquieted by the quiet, Mrs. Watson looked up from her meal.

"You should hear what Gracie told me today," she said. "She is so precious."

Mr. Watson ran a hand over his face. He took a deep breath. Out of the corner of his eye, he noticed patrons at nearby tables lean over to gossip with one another.

"Do tell," he said. Not wishing to worsen the matter by calling her out on such a delicate matter in such a public place, he listened patiently, but then and there, Mr. Watson resolved to remove Mrs. Watson from this disconcerting un-reality.

A week later, Mr. Watson accepted a job at the DeSoto, just a few blocks away. A grand sprawling hotel, he thought, at the very least, he would be so busy with his work that he would be able to set aside his troubled thoughts — at least during the workday.

As the movers loaded the Watson's belongings onto the carriage, Mrs. Watson sat in silence upon a parlor chair she had dragged under the stairs.

Outside, in Johnson Square, Mr. Watson was supervising the movers. He pulled his pocket watch from his vest. He sighed. He knew this was to be no easy task, moving his bereaved wife out of the hotel. He stuffed the watch back in his vest pocket and marched into the hotel.

Mr. Watson strode down the hallway, bracing himself for the worst. As he rounded the corner, he could hear Miss Mathilda talking with his wife.

"Don't you worry," said Miss Mathilda. "I'll take good care of Miss Gracie.... Have I ever let you down before?"

Has the world gone mad?

He realized that Miss Mathilda was merely placating Mrs. Watson, coaxing her to leave peacefully.

Mrs. Watson had a difficult time adjusting to her new surroundings. Every so often, a runner would come by and ask Mr. Watson to come and remove his wife from under the stairs at the back of the Pulaski House. Each time he did so, he feigned an eagerness to listen to his wife reminisce over her discussions with their late daughter. It was the only way to return her to her new home. He thought he'd thought of everything, until an old friend moved to town.

John Walz was a sculptor of some renown. His life-like creations were always wonders to behold. Mr. Watson thought, perhaps, if he could simply create a statue of Gracie to mark her grave at Bonaventure, then maybe, just maybe, his wife would find some peace.

He rummaged through the trunk that still held some of Gracie's things. There, at the bottom, was the only photograph of their daughter. He had buried it there. The faded image of his daughter wrenched his heart.

Without a word, he climbed into the carriage and silently rode off to Mr. Walz's studio, just outside of town. As he rode, he tried to think of how best to explain what he wanted. After all, he was no sculptor, only a hotel manager. What could he possibly say?

He slowed the carriage to a stop in front of Walz's studio. He could hear the clanking of metal on stone, and the crumbling of marble as it hit the floor. He sighed. Then, he stepped on to the carriage block and tied the reigns to the hitching post. He reached up, stretching to snag the framed photograph from the leather bench seat in the carriage. With all the courage he could muster, he slowly ambled into the studio.

Mr. Walz was chiseling away at a large block of Georgia marble when Mr. Watson entered his studio. He looked up from his work. He could see that Mr. Watson was distressed. Rather than shatter the silence, John Walz nodded to his friend.

Mr. Watson approached timidly. He could feel his chest tighten. Tears welled in his eyes. With trembling hand, he presented Mr. Walz with the only image of his daughter, Gracie. The men nodded, and Mr. Watson silently left the studio.

Some months later, Mr. Walz informed Mr. Watson that the statue was finished. Mr. Watson excused himself from his duties at the DeSoto and rushed over, hoping not so much to inspect the work, but to lay eyes upon his daughter's likeness, lest he forget.

Mr. Walz lay a calloused hand upon the sheet covering the statue. He looked Mr. Watson squarely in the eye. Mr. Watson nodded. The sheet fell from the statue, revealing a beautiful, flawless, life-size, and lifelike image of little Gracie, sitting upon a rock, with her hand resting gently upon the stump of a young birch.

Mr. Watson's eyes fell upon her serene expression. His lip quivered. Months of putting on a brave face for the world to see came to a head, and there, in the studio of John Walz, Mr. Watson wept, his head resting upon the shoulder of his daughter.

The next day, the Watson's rode out to Bonaventure. Mrs. Watson was silent all the way. She saw no need to visit that beautiful but dreadful place. It held nothing for her.

The carriage entered the gate, and Mr. Watson slowed the horses to a gentle amble. They rode beneath a canopy of majestic, moss-covered oaks, passing rows of those in eternal slumber. He held the reigns in one hand, and took his wife's hand with the other.

"I want to show you something," he said. He pulled up on the reigns, slowing the horses to a gentle stop just in front of Gracie's grave. Mrs. Watson would not look up.

"Why have you brought me here?" she said, with her head bowed.

"Because Gracie is here, and will always be here."

Mrs. Watson looked into her husband's gentle eyes. He nodded. Mrs. Watson looked over her shoulder and saw little Gracie, in her splendid formal dress, waiting for her mother. Mrs. Watson buried her face in her husband's shoulder. The grief, the agony that had been simmering for nearly a year exploded in the solitude of the cemetery. She clutched at his coat. Her fists beat against his chest. She wailed.

And then, there was silence....

There, under the canopy of oaks that shade the slumbering souls, Mr. Watson held his wife close, and wept along with her.

The strain of losing Gracie was too much to bear for the Watson's. Eventually, they packed their bags and left Savannah, never to return.

Rumors of Gracie's presence persist to this day. On the site of the Pulaski House (Bull and Bryan, on Johnson Square) locals contend they've seen — through the windows of what was once the Piccadilly Cafeteria (and is now a bank) — a little girl in a Victorian dress. Others claim to have seen this same little girl run by them when they were either visiting the cafeteria, or standing near the southwest corner of the building.

As to the rumors of glowing statues and the like, paranormal researchers agree that the dearly departed tend not to haunt their graves, but instead linger at the places where they met their early passing. Other spirits return to the place they loved very much. Little Gracie, hostess of the Pulaski House, is a rare spirit who fits both categories.

Her statue is located in Bonaventure Cemetery in Section E, Lot 99.

Bo-Cat

Pin Point, Georgia (near Savannah), 1932

Catherine smiled as she placed the daisies in the crooked clay flowerpot. It didn't much matter that it leaned a little too much to the side, or looked like it was wilting from the hot Georgia sun. She just loved the way the golden daisies looked against the terra cotta painted haint blue. Besides that, she had made it with her own hands a day or two before she married Bo-Cat, combining "something new" with "something blue."

She sighed.

Things weren't right between her and Bo-Cat, and hadn't been for a long, long time. While she loved their tiny little house in Pin Point, Bo-Cat always seemed to want something more. Seems he was always trying to find the easy way out of hard times, but it was 1932; everyone around them was poor.

She placed the flowers on the windowsill and took a moment to admire them.

"Catherine!"

Catherine opened the door and half-skipped her way into the waiting arms of her friend, Miss Margaret.

"How you been, baby?" said Margaret, warmly.

"I'm okay," she replied, taking Margaret's hand. "Come wit' me while I fix a pitchuh of ice watuh fo' Limerick."

The ladies stepped through a creaky screen door and into the tiny kitchen. Margaret took a moment to look at the spring on the door.

"Ain't he fixed this yet?" she said, working the door back and forth.

Catherine pulled a heavy glass pitcher off the shelf and set it on the counter, and then grabbed a block of ice out of the icebox.

"I don't know why you fixin' this ice watuh," said Margaret as she rummaged through the drawer for an ice pick. "It's not like he workin'."

"He tryin' to find work," said Catherine.

"He oughta be spendin' mo' time 'round here," said Margaret, methodically chipping away the block of ice.

Catherine stepped out of the house, pitcher in hand, and strode over to the water pump. After a few squeaky cranks of the handle, the water flowed freely. She waited until the water was clear before half-filling the pitcher. When she closed the valve, she heard the screen door slap shut.

Margaret scurried over to the pitcher with her hands full of ice.

"Ooh! Cold!" she said, dumping the uneven shards into the pitcher.

Catherine found herself staring down the winding road that connected Pin Point to Savannah.

"Why don't you come to town wit' me to-mawrah?" said Margaret. "Just us ladies."

"I don't know," said Catherine, wiping her brow. "Limerick wants me to stay here."

"That's why we should go," said Margaret. Catherine thought about it for a moment, and then laughed.

"You a mess," she said.

Margaret and Catherine looked up and saw Bo-Cat stomping down the path. Margaret watched as the smile faded from Catherine's face.

"Hey, Bo-Cat," said Miss Margaret.

Bo-Cat flashed a sharp, dismissive wave. Catherine noticed Margaret's raised eyebrows, and put a gentle hand on her shoulder.

"Don't," said Catherine. "You'll only set him off."

"Oh, I'll set him off, alright," she said. "Mm-hmm.

"I'll see you to-mawruh," said Margaret.

Catherine hugged Margaret with one arm, so as not to spill the ice water. Then, she walked over to the house, and let herself in through that creaky screen door. She could hear Limerick rummaging through a box in the cramped bedroom.

"Made you some ice watuh, baby," she said, softly. "It's been sittin' just long enough, so it's nice an' cold."

Without looking at his wife, Bo-Cat said, "Where's my deed?"

"Why do you need the deed, baby?" said Catherine.

"Jus' do," he snapped. "Now, where is it?"

Catherine could feel the knot in her stomach. She knew the tears wouldn't be too far behind. Quietly, she stepped back and set the glass pitcher on a plate on the counter. Then, trembling, she returned to the small, dark room where Bo-Cat searched for the papers.

"Do you want me to help you?" she asked, gently.

Bo-Cat glared at her over his shoulder. Suddenly, he slammed the box down. Catherine jumped. She slowly backed out of the room and let her husband pass. Bo-Cat slid by and moved toward the screen door. Catherine drew her arms close to her body, her fingers resting on her lips. She jumped again as Bo-Cat burst through the door with such force that it snapped the spring. Slowly, Catherine slid down the wall, dropped her head to her knees, and began sobbing.

Catherine padded across the uneven floor to water the daisies. As she raised the pitcher closer to the vase, the golden flowers shriveled, turning black. She stepped back, shivering. The pitcher felt heavy — too heavy — so she set it on the counter. As she did, she noticed that, instead of ice water, the pitcher was filled with thick, black muck. Suddenly, the flowers swayed, though the air in the room was stagnant. With trembling hands, she reached for the flowers. As she pulled the dead stems from the vase, a coral snake coiled in the bottom of the flowerpot lashed at her. The haint blue vase tumbled to the floor, shattering on impact.

Catherine woke to the sound of the slamming door. She watched as Bo-Cat, silhouetted against the early morning light, stomped off to who-knows-where.

Margaret and Catherine walked down Barnard Street to Ellis Square. They knew they weren't allowed to shop in most stores in downtown Savannah, but there were a few shops here and there where they could spend what little money they had. Mostly, though, they wandered through City Market, hoping to find some fresh fruit. Most folks in the Point did their own gardening. The men would hunt possum or do a little fishing, so their needs were well met. Still, nobody could grow oranges, and it was a real treat when the farmers from Florida showed up with a truckload of the colorful fruit.

As they wandered past the stalls, Catherine told Margaret of her dream.

"Oh, chile," said Margaret. "You know what they say when you dream about snakes. You have a' enemy."

Margaret tapped an orange and frowned. She placed the overripe fruit at the top of the crate and dusted off her hands.

"I know," said Catherine.

"Whatcha goin' to do 'bout it?" Margaret said.

"Ain't nothin' I can do 'bout it," said Catherine. "'cept keep an eye on him.

"Worse part 'bout it," she said, "it's a double bad luck day"

Margaret looked at Catherine. *It's Friday, the thirteenth.*

By the time Margaret and Catherine made their way back to Pin Point, the sun was dipping below the tree line. As they walked along the path, Margaret found herself staring into the moss-draped canopy above.

"I love the way the sunlight shines through the moss like that," she said. "It sho' is pretty."

Margaret noticed that Catherine was limping along.

"You okay, baby?" she asked.

"It's nothin'," Catherine said. "Jus' this ol' cawn actin' up 'gain."

"You had that forevuh," said Margaret.

Catherine heard the rhythmic metallic scraping of something being sharpened. She turned white.

"What's the matter?" said Margaret.

"It's Limerick," she said. "He's home already, and he's mad."

"How you know that?" Margaret asked.

"He only takes to sharp'nin' when he's mad," she said.

Margaret gently took Catherine by the arm and the two ladies walked toward the tiny house.

"Hey, Bo-Cat," said Margaret, completely unphased by the brooding Bo-Cat.

"Best git on home, Miss Margaret," said Limerick, dragging a stone across the blade of the hoe. "Me an' Catherine got some talkin' to do."

"Limerick, I asked her to go wit' me," she said. "So you can do your talkin' to me!"

Bo-Cat jumped to his feet, clutching the sharpened hoe. Catherine quietly leaned over and whispered in Miss Margaret's ear.

"It's okay, Margaret," said Catherine. "I'll be alright."

Bo-Cat watched as Margaret walked down the path leading to her house. When he was sure that she was out of sight, he seized Catherine by the arms and pulled her close.

"Where you been all day?" he snarled.

The sack holding the fresh fruit burst open. The few oranges she could afford tumbled to the ground. Limerick looked down.

"You wastin' my money on fruit?" he growled.

Bo-Cat gripped Catherine by the arm and dragged her to the house. As they got closer, he shoved her through the open screen door. She stumbled, and fell hard against the rickety kitchen table. The legs snapped off, and she tumbled to the ground, her head butting against the icebox. Punch drunk from the fall, Catherine tried to claw her way to the door. Bo-Cat snatched a leg from the table and, wielding it like a club, struck her hard across the back. Catherine collapsed from the force of the blow.

He seized her by the ankle and dragged her down to the rowboat. A moan escaped Catherine's lips as Bo-Cat dumped her body in the boat. With a grunt, he shoved off. Down the Black River he rowed, all the way to Hell's Gate.

When he came to Raccoon Keys, Bo-Cat beached the boat. He stepped into the marshy water and slogged his way to the shore. When the rowboat was secure enough, he seized Catherine by the collar and dragged her out of the boat and along the shoreline until he came across an old, fallen tree. There, he dropped her body, and returned to the rowboat. Just as he was climbing into the boat, he heard a scurrying sound. Bo-Cat turned around to see Catherine struggling to her feet. He snatched an oar and stalked over to her, the oar raised over his head. He watched as his wife tried to scuttle away from him — and then brought the oar down hard upon her.

Bo-Cat looked at the splintered oar and cussed.

Weeks later....

Margaret and her brother, Saul, sat on the porch, staring out at the river. Folks in Pin Point hardly slept, some hoping for Catherine's return, most fearing the worst, none believing that such a thing could happen to sweet Catherine.

"Leas' they 'rested Lim'rick," said Saul. "I hear they gonna hang 'im."

Margaret rocked quietly.

"I s'pose that'll be hard to do if they don' find the body," he continued.

"They found it, all right," said Margaret. "Leas' what's left of it."

"How you know?" said Saul.

"She have this nasty cawn on the bottom uh her foot," Margaret said. "Never could git rid of it...."

Saul looked at his sister. He knew she was the one who could have identified poor Catherine's body — and the only one who would have remembered something so small as a corn on the bottom of her foot.

On a rainy Monday, people from all around packed the Sweet Field of Eden Church. The tiny church overflowed with mourners hoping to pay their last respects to a fine, upstanding woman.

When the strains of "Soon One Morning" faded into a quiet hum, folks knew it was their time to share their thoughts on Catherine.

"Catherine DeLancy was a sistuh of the Lawd," cried a voice from the back of the church.

"She sho' was," cried another voice.

"I know that's right," said another.

"She was a chile o' Jesus," called out another.

Nearly a hundred people gave testimony about Catherine's goodness, and of the tragedy of her death, right up until the time when the preacher gave the signal to move the procession to the tiny cemetery.

Slowly, the congregation filed out and formed a double receiving line in front of the church. When the deacon saw the minister leading the pallbearers out of the church, he started singing.

"I'm troubled! I'm troubled! I'm troubled in mind!" he sang. Soon, the congregation sang along, falling in behind the pallbearers. Down to the cemetery they walked, swaying to the rhythm of that long, slow hymn.

"If the Good Lord won't help me, I surely would die...."

At the grave, each member of the congregation took a handful of dirt and threw it on the coffin. It wasn't long before just about everyone had said their peace and gone home. Miss Margaret, Saul, and a few others stayed around until the diggers filled in the grave. Once the mound was finished, each placed something on the grave that meant something to Catherine in life: some perfume bottles, a lamp chimney, even the pitcher she used to make Bo-Cat his ice water. The last thing Miss Margaret placed on the grave was that old flowerpot, painted haint blue.

Miss Margaret Snead, of Pin Point, Georgia, provided the testimonial for this tale in the late 1930s. She contends that Catherine's spirit will never rest in the grave because the poor woman was "denied of all the proper things that come for burial."

Hag Ridden

Savannah, 1938

Clay felt the weight bearing down on his chest.

Not again, he thought. *Dear Lord, not again.*

He tried to call to his wife, sleeping next to him, but he could barely force a breathless murmur through his lips. He tried to force himself to sit up or perhaps beat on the bed to get her attention, but he could barely wiggle his toes. His breathing became shallow and sullen, and in his last waking moments, he felt the hot breath of the hag.

Clay-y-y-y-y

"Clay?" said Lila. Her voice was soothing, yet insistent.

"Clay, baby. You're going to be late for work."

Clay stirred, and then sat bolt upright.

"What time is it?" he said, trying to get his bearings.

"Almost nine."

"Damn it!" Clay tumbled out of bed and began rummaging for his overalls.

"I have everything right here, baby," said Lila.

"Why didn't you wake me?" said Clay, fumbling with straps and buckles.

"Clay," said Lila, arms folded tight across her chest. "I spent the last hour trying to wake you. Didn't you hear me?"

"Guess not," he replied, forcing his foot into a big, rubber boot.

"I even gave you a little shove," she said. "Now, take your lunch and get on out the door!"

Clay yarded the weathered door open and stepped out onto what passed for a porch. As he was closing the door, Lila caught the edge.

"Ain't you gonna kiss me goodbye?" she said with a smirk. Clay smiled and gave her a solid peck on the lips. When he opened his eyes, he saw that Lila's mouth was twisted into a brooding pout.

"What, baby?" Clay said. Lila responded with a sharp, upward nod.

"Malinda," said Lila, glaring at the woman across the street. "I know she ridin' you."

"Aw, no!" said Clay. "When would she and I — "

Lila snatched Clay's cap off his head and smacked him hard across the top of his head.

"Not like that, fool!" said Lila, shoving the threadbare cap into Clay's chest. "That woman is a hag! A hag, I tell you! That's why you ain't been sleepin' right!

"Now, get yo'se'f to work befo' you lose your job!"

Clay slapped the cap on his head and shuffled down the rickety steps. As he walked down Perry

Street, he glanced over his shoulder to see Malinda Edmonde slide back into her tiny apartment.

"She give me the creeps, too!"

Clay flinched.

"Easy boy," said the wiry man, keeping pace with Clay. A very eager Redbone Coonhound was pulling him along.

"Mis-tah Holmes," said Clay with a smile. "Hoo, Lord, you lookin' as ragged as me."

S.B. Holmes was always a little lean, but these days, he seemed especially skinny, his face looking drawn and thin, with deep bags under his eyes.

"I ain't been getting' much sleep," he said. "I think I been rid by the hag."

Clay stopped in his tracks.

"My wife, she say the same thing 'bout me!"

"I saw her givin' the eye to ol' Malinda Edmonde," said S.B. He fished into his pocket, dug out a piece of dried beef, and offered it to the hound.

"Mm-hmm," said Clay, resuming his walk. "Scared me though. I thought fo' sho she believed Melinda an' me was carryin' on."

S.B. busted out chuckling. He laughed so hard he had to stop to catch his breath.

"What?" said Clay.

"I don't know which makes me laugh harder," he said. "That you'd be foolish enough to cheat on Lila, or that Malinda would actually be desperate enough carry on with the likes ah you!"

Clay paused… then chortled.

"That would be desperate!"

The men parted ways at East Broad Street, and Clay headed off to the stables.

Clay found his mind wandering. He used to mock the old folks when they told stories of hags and witches — and who could blame him? After all, who could believe that a woman could slip out of her skin? Or dissolve into a mist? Or change into a cat? And if that weren't believable enough, such a woman would go through all that trouble to steal the life's breath right out of another — and by riding his chest in the middle of the night, too! Unbelievable!

And yet, it was happening to him, and to Mr. Holmes, too!

Clay slid open the stable door. He could hear Mr. Tully cussing under his breath.

"Mr. Tully?" Clay said, warily. "You alright?"

"The horses had night sweats — all of 'em!" Tully said, mopping his brow with his hairy forearm. He dipped the brush into the bucket of cool, soapy water and continued bathing the stallion.

"Grab that comb and see if you can't get these knots out of his mane."

Clay froze.

"Did you hear me?"

Clay shook it off, snatched up the brush, and began grooming the mount's mane.

"If I didn't know any better, I'd say we have a witch, right here in Savannah!" said Tully, ringing out the sponge.

Clay stopped.

"What did you say?" said Clay. He felt as if all his energy had just run out his body.

"A witch," Tully replied. "When I was growin' up in County Down, I'd hear stories about mischievous witches and of how they would drive cattle from the barns and steal food from the mouths of babes. You could always tell when one was nearby, because the horses would wake up in the sweat of the mornin' — and they always had these knots in their manes."

"Hag stirrups," Clay whispered.

"We used to hang a horseshoe above the door, to keep 'em away," said Tully, running a hand through a shock of red hair. "I'll have to nail up one or two here, as well, I suppose."

After work, Clay wandered down to visit old Jack Wilson. Jack ran a tumbledown junk shop on McAlister Street, but everyone in Old Fort knew Jack had the ability to see spirits and talk with the dead. Some Geechee believed it was because Jack was born with a caul, but Jack, a deep-rooted Geechee himself, would never own up to it.

Clay meandered through the stacks of sacks and scrap iron and found Jack squatting in the modest vegetable garden, pulling weeds. Jack paused long enough to glance over his shoulder.

"You have duh look of uh ridden man," said Jack.

"Yes, sir," said Clay, hat in hand.

Jack tossed the weeds into a rusty drum and dusted off his hands. He then tottered into his tin shack. A moment later, he emerged with a weathered bible.

"You need religion, boy," Jack said, offering the bible to Clay.

"But I have a bible," said Clay, refusing the offer.

"Den, you need tuh put it unduh yo' pilluh," said Jack. "Dat'll keep duh witch away fo' sho.'"

Jack then fished in his pocket and pulled out a silver dime. He shuffled over to a makeshift anvil, grabbed an eight-penny nail, and drove a hole through the dime. Looking around, he spotted a spool of waxed thread. He pulled a short length, snipped it and threaded it through the hole.

"Give dis to yo' wife," he said. "Have huh wear it 'round huh ankle. An' if you have uh pinny, nail it to yo' do'step; mebbe ev'n lay a broom 'cross duh t'resh-ho'd at night."

Clay stood dumbfounded.

"'Til you kin find duh witch," he said. "Dese should offuh some protection."

But Clay wasn't interested in protection. He wanted to catch the hag.

The next day, Clay walked on over to S.B.'s house. He rapped on the door, and when S.B. opened it, he handed the man a horseshoe.

"What's this fo'?" asked S.B. as he studied the horseshoe.

"Protection," said Clay. "From the hag. Tully say to nail it above your do', so the hag can't come through. An' Mister Wilson, he say to put a bible under your pillow."

"I ain't putting no bible under my pillow," said S.B. "I just don't feel right about that."

"Then lay a broom 'cross your do'."

"Okay," he said. "That I can do!"

"What about you?"

"I been thinkin' 'bout this all day," said Clay. "I s'pect that if I put the bible under my pillow, like Mr. Wilson say, the hag will leave me alone."

"And?"

Clay fiddled with the frayed edges of his cap, almost embarrassed to look up at S.B.

"Then, I figure she'll need to ride somebody...."

"Aw, no, Clay!" said S.B. "You ain't — "

"How you 'spect me to catch her?" he said.

"All I know is, if Lila ever finds out you been usin' her as bait," said S.B. "You gonna catch a whole lot more than some nasty ol' hag!"

"That's where you come in, Espy."

Hours passed....

Clay stared at the ceiling. As he listened to his wife's breathing, he hoped he wasn't making a terrible mistake. He began to wonder whether he shouldn't just tie the dime around his wife's ankle like Mr. Wilson said, or slip the bible that rested beneath his pillow under hers.

All this talk of witches and hags made him realize just how dangerous this game was. He remembered Tully's story of a time long ago when a small village in Ireland lost many of their first born to a boo-hag. It all came to a bloody end when a farmer found his only son being suffocated by a black cat....

Then, he felt it: a soft, gentle breeze wafting over him! *But how?* He had closed the windows, hadn't he? Suddenly, the axe handle he brought to bed with him was of little comfort.

Clay shut his eyes tight, and clutched the axe handle tighter. He waited....

He felt the bed move. *Lila?* No. Lila lay still.

Clay froze. His heart raced. *Was that a shadow?*

Then, he heard a soft moan escape Lila's lips. He felt her fingers wiggling. He knew. The hag was in their bed!

Clay jumped to his feet, swinging the axe handle wildly at the shadows, hoping to knock the hag off his wife. A blood-curdling screech echoed in the darkness, and Clay saw the shadow disappear into the black of night.

Still in his nightshirt, clutching the axe handle, Clay bolted out the door. He sprinted over to S.B.'s house. He beat on the door.

The old hound began baying long before Clay arrived, and S.B. was ready.

"I hit her!" said Clay, holding out the axe handle. "With this."

S.B. let the dog sniff the handle, and soon they were on the trail.

"Look like paw prints!" said S.B. "Maybe a cat!"

The cat seemed to traipse through a mud puddle, but the prints disappeared. The hound, however, wasn't giving up.

"You see that?!" said Clay.

"Footprints!" S.B. crossed himself. "Lord, a slip-skin!"

S.B.'s hound strained against the leash, pulling the men into the underbrush. Suddenly, the Redbone started snarling and barking at the undergrowth. Cautiously, Clay parted the branches with the axe handle. There, pressed up against the fence corner, clutching her ribs and breathing hard, was a nude Malinda Edmonde.

"Please," she said, wincing. "Please, don't hit me no mo'. I'll leave you alone. I promise…."

Admittedly, this story defies logic and reason, but this author knows better than to argue with the old folks who hold it dear to their hearts.

No Mo' Mojo

Summer 1945

The rickety pickup rumbled down the shell-laden road, past tin shacks and broken-down autos. As he rolled up on the ramshackle bungalow, John Burden started having second thoughts. Ah, if only he had second thoughts the first time he visited ol' Doctor Buzzard....

John killed the engine and waited for the truck to sputter out. He dropped his head and blew out a long, slow breath, relieved that he made it in one piece. He turned his gaze to the small sachet that rested on the dashboard. Only God knew what dark magic that little bundle possessed — God, and men like Doctor Buzzard.

John flinched. Out of the corner of his eye, he saw Doc Buzzard leaning against the hant blue porch post, puffing peacefully on his pipe. John gingerly picked up the packet, pinching the fraying edge like the tail of a dead rat. He creaked open the door to the pickup, stepped out and greeted Doc Buzzard with a sharp nod. Without so much as a wave, the good doctor casually rolled off the post and sauntered into the bungalow.

Truth was, nobody but Doc Buzzard (and God) knew his real name. Odds were pretty good that the man himself had been practicing under that moniker for so long, even he had a hard time remembering his birth name. (It's probably a good thing, too, since the D.A. never took too kindly to the doctor's practice. While folks along coastal Georgia called it, "root work" or "hoodoo" or "mojo" or "conjurin'," the State called it, "practicing without a license.")

The screen door snapped shut. John jumped, and then sighed. He looked around the cramped room. A hodgepodge of bunched and bundled herbs hung upside down in the window above the sink. Jugs, jars, and bottles with odd labels cluttered the cabinets. Nothing had changed since his last visit a year ago.

The beaded curtains parted with a rattle. John swallowed hard. Ol' Doc Buzzard shuffled to the roughhewn desk in the middle of the room.

"What's got you so jumpy, boy?" he said in a croaky voice. Doc Buzzard eased himself into a creaky chair. Without looking at John, he raised a hand as an invitation to sit.

John pulled up a short three-legged stool and squatted. He felt foolish, hunkered down on that tiny stool.

"Well?" said Doc, peering over his reading glasses. John's head and shoulders barely rose above the edge of the desk. That's the way Doc liked it. With the patient perched precariously on the tiny stool and he, himself, raised up on the high-backed chair, it gave the good doctor an edge — at least psychologically.

John stretched to set the sachet on the desk. Doc Buzzard snatched it up and examined it carefully.

"Where did you find this?" he asked.

"In my pillow," he replied.

"*In* your pillow? Or *under* your pillow?"

"In my pillow," said John.

"Hmmm," said the doctor, untying the twine that bundled the packet. He opened the sachet and laid it flat on the desk. He took a pencil and carefully picked through the contents: nail trimmings, a bit of hair, a piece of cloth, dried herbs, and some dirt.

"In your pillow...." Doc said. He jotted down a few notes in his journal. When he finished writing, he stared at John.

"What is it?" said John, with a dry swallow.

"You cheatin' on your woman." It wasn't a question. John shifted uncomfortably on the stool. "Question is," said Doc, still staring at John. "Which woman?"

"I don't —"

"You lied to me," said Dr. Buzzard.

"I swear! I found it in my damn pillow!"

"Don't you cuss at me," said Doc. "I ain't talkin' 'bout no damn pillow. You came in here last year and asked me to mix you up some attraction powder for this woman you liked. Guess you forgot to tell me that you was already married!"

John dropped his head.

"Yeah. I thought so," said Doc. "I don't appreciate bein' used, Mister John."

"How you know?"

Doc Buzzard stood up and gazed out the window. He cocked his head toward to the splayed open sachet.

"It's all right there, young man," he said. "Your wife wants you to stop foolin' 'round."

"But I can't sleep!" said John. "I'm tired all the time. I can't concentrate."

"And your dirty little dreams have become nasty nightmares," Doc said.

"Yes," said John, staring at his hands.

"So you want the other woman to go away?" Doc asked as he rifled through a drawer or two. "I can do that."

"No," said John.

"No?" said Doc. "Oh, really?

"Why are you here, Mr. John?" Doc leaned heavily on the cluttered desk. "So I can help you with your affair?"

"I just want to sleep!"

"Then you don't need me, Mr. John," said Doc. "You need to walk away from the other woman and make up with your wife!"

"But the hex?" John asked. "What about the hex?"

Doc sat down and jotted a number on a scrap of paper. He then carefully slid it across the desk toward John. John looked at the number and couldn't help but gasp. While Doc busied himself with powders and potions, John reached into his pocket, pulled out a wad of small bills, and set it in the middle of the desk. Since root doctors couldn't legally charge a fee for their services, Doc would leave the money there and wouldn't pick it up until John drove away. This little ritual protected Doc, and his clients, from diligent District Attorneys.

Doc Buzzard returned to the desk with a purple flannel sachet, and a tiny glass jar. He set each in front of John.

"Now, pay attention," said Doc, holding up the sachet. "You keep this with you night and day, and keep it dry." He offered the sachet to John.

"Take it, boy!" said Doc. "This one ain't gonna hurt you."

John took the bag.

"Now," said Doc, holding up the little jar. "This is your feeding powder."

"Feeding powder?"

"Yes," Doc said. "This sack has a *mooyo*. It is alive. You have to feed it once a week — and always at day-clean on Sunday!"

"How do I —"

"Stop interruptin'," said Doc. "You jus' sprinkle a little of it o'er what's inside that purple sack. Do this every week."

"On Sundays," said John with a nod.

"On Sundays," Doc replied. "'Til it's gone — an' don' let anyone know you carryin' this."

"How long?"

"'Til it's gone." Doc craned his neck around to look at the calendar tacked to the wall. "Pro'ly May."

"May?!?" said John. "That's three months from now!"

"And it's gonna take you a long time to undo what you done," said Doc.

"What I done?" said John. "I ain't the one who hexed me."

"No," said Doc. "But your actions caused you to be rooted. You dippin' your wick in another woman's wax caused the conjurin', and unless you want her to step it up, you stop your cheatin'.."

Dr. Buzzard escorted John to the door. He paused a moment before pushing the screen door open.

"Mr. John," said Doc, staring hard into John's eyes. "This will be the last time I help you. If she roots you again, you're on your own."

John swallowed hard, and then shuffled toward his weather-beaten pickup.

Ol' Doc Buzzard leaned against the hant blue porch post and puffed on his pipe. He could see the rickety old pickup rumbling down the road. He frowned.

Oh no he didn't, thought Doc. *I know he's not comin' here.*

The pickup shuddered to a stop. When the dust cleared, Doc smiled. He scrambled off the porch and hustled over to the beat up truck.

"Mrs. Burden!" He laughed as he hugged the husky woman. "When I saw the truck, I thought for sure you was John. Sure am glad it's you!"

Mrs. Burden smiled.

"I need to talk with you," she said, the smile fading from her face. Doc Buzzard took her by the hand and the two walked along the marsh like they were long, lost friends.

"The root didn't take?"

"The one for me? Or the one you prescribed for John?"

Doc smiled. "You know I can't talk about another patient."

"Look. I know you tried to help us," she said. "And I appreciate that, but John's always been a little... selfish."

"So he's still cheating on you?" Doc said. He tapped his pipe on the palm of his hand, loosening the last of the tobacco.

"No," said Mrs. Burden. "I divorced his ass after he left me for that other woman!"

"I'm sorry to hear that," said Doc.

"Not your fault," she said. "At least I got the truck, and the house!"

They laughed heartily.

"But what's even better is that other root you gave."

"The one that keeps him from, 'performin'?" said Doc with a wink.

"Yes sir," beamed Mrs. Burden. "After a couple of weeks of not pleasin' her, she kicked him to the curb, now he beggin' me to take him back!"

"You gonna reconcile?"

"You crazy?!" she said slapping his shoulder. "Not only is he lazy, but he can't even make love no mo'. What woman wants that? He on his own!"

"Root Work" or "Hoodoo" is a rich and complex tradition, which can be traced back to the heart of Africa. There are still dozens — if not hundreds — of practitioners who use "conjuring" to help others. Until his death in 1947, Doctor Buzzard, the most famous of these, practiced root work

in the Low Country of South Carolina, and throughout the Coastal Empire of Georgia, traveling as far south as the Golden Isles. "No Mo' Mojo" is a blending of testimonials, happenings, and anecdotal tales. This story is inspired by those who work the root, and by those who believe wholeheartedly in its power to change lives — for better or for worse.

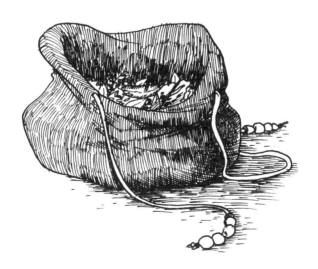

Bibliography

Bailey, Cornelia Walker. 2000. *God, Dr. Buzzard and the Bolito Man: A Saltwater Geechee Talks about Life on Sapelo Island, Georgia.* New York: Anchor Books.

Berendt, John. 1994. *Midnight in the Garden of Good and Evil.* New York: Random House, Inc.

Bird, Stephanie Rose. 2004. *Sticks, Stones, Roots and Bones: Hoodoo, Mojo and Conjuring with Herbs.* St. Paul: Llewellyn Publications.

Caskey, James. 2005. *Haunted Savannah: The Official Guidebook to Savannah Haunted History Tour.* Savannah: Bonaventure Books.

Cobb, Al. 2003. *Savannah's Ghosts II.* Savannah: Whitaker Street Press.

Coffey, Tom. 1994. *Only in Savannah: Stories and Insights on Georgia's Mother City.* Savannah: Frederic C. Beil, Publisher.

Courlander, Harold. 1976. *A Treasury of Afro-American Folklore.* New York: Marlowe and Company.

Daise, Ronald. 1986. *Reminiscences of Sea Island Heritage.* Orangeburg, SC: Sandlapper Publishing, Inc.

Daiss, Timothy. 2002. *Rebels, Saints, and Sinners.* Savannah: Pelican Publishing Company.

DeBolt, Margaret Wayt. 1984. *Savannah Spectres and Other Strange Tales.* Virginia Beach, VA: The Donning Company.

Dick, Susan E. and Mandi D. Johnson. 2001. *Savannah: 1733 to 2000.* Charleston, SC: Arcadia Publishing.

Fraser, Walter J. 2003. *Savannah in the Old South.* Athens, GA: University of Georgia Press.

Gamble, Thomas. 1923. *Savannah Duels and Duellists: 1733-1877*. Savannah: Review Publishing and Printing Co.

Georgia Writer's Project. 1940. *Drums and Shadows: Survival Stories Among The Georgia Coastal Negroes*. Athens, GA: University of Georgia Press.

Johnson, Wittington B. 1996. *Black Savannah*. Fayetteville: University of Arkansas Press.

Lane, Mills. 2001. *Savannah Revisited: History & Architecture, 5th Edition*. Savannah: The Beehive Press.

Pinckney, Roger. 1998. *Blue Roots: African-American Folk Magic of the Gullah People*. St. Paul: Llewellyn Publications.

Russell, Preston and Barbara Hines. 1992. *Savannah: A History of Her People Since 1733*. Savannah: Frederic C. Beil, Publisher.

Smith, Derek. 1997. *Civil War Savannah*. Savannah: Frederic C. Beil, Publisher.

Toledano, Roulhac. 1997. *The National Trust Guide to Savannah Architectural & Cultural Treasures*. New York: John Wiley & Sons.

Turnage, Sheila. 2001. *Haunted Inns of the Southeast*. Winston-Salem, NC: John F. Blair, Publisher.

Wilson, Amie Marie and Mandi D. Johnson. 1998. *Historic Bonaventure Cemetery*. Charleston, SC: Arcadia Publishing.

Yetman, Norman R., ed. 1970. *Voices for Slavery: 100 Authentic Slave Narratives*. New York: Holt, Rinehart, and Winston, Inc.

MORE SCHIFFER TITLES
www.schifferbooks.com

Ghosts! Washington Revisited: The Ghostlore of the Nation's Capitol. John Alexander. A reporter for the capitol's Washington Star newspaper wrote in 1891, "Washington is the greatest town for ghosts in this country." John Alexander has collected and preserved tales about the famous and infamous of the nation's capitol who still revisit the White House, the U.S. Capitol, and many other buildings and homes said to be haunted. Ghosts! Washington Revisited is a revised and updated edition of Ghosts! Washington's Most Famous Ghost Stories. Among these tales are ghost stories from neighboring Virginia and Maryland communities including Mount Vernon, Arlington, Alexandria, Manassas, and the Blandensburg dueling grounds. These spectral tales are accompanied by over 180 images of haunted sites and famous individuals said to return to Washington long after departing this life.

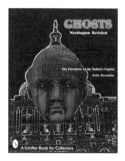

Size: 8 1/2" x 11"   180+ b/w photographs and illustrations   128 pp.
ISBN: 0-7643-0653-7   soft cover $14.95

Creepy Colleges and Haunted Universities: True Ghost Stories. Cynthia Thuma & Catherine Lower. College ghosts are a little like college mascots – just about every school has one and they add a dash of spice to the college experience. Drawn from across North America, coast to coast, here's a directory of ghosts, spirits, specters, and apparitions who haunt educational institutions from small community colleges to great universities. This collection of terrifying tales and alarming anecdotes relates more than 140 schools' eerie experiences with the afterlife. It includes the the mischevious ghost of George Gipp, University of Notre Dame's legendary football hero, and the quiet, restless ghost of playwright Eugene O'Neill in Boston University's Shelton Hall. It is guaranteed to send a chill up your spine and keep you up late.

Size: 6" x 9"   23 b/w photos   128 pp.
ISBN: 0-7643-1805-5   soft cover $16.95

California Ghosts: True Accounts of Hauntings in the Golden State. Preston E. Dennett. Do you believe in ghosts? Have you ever seen one? This chilling volume presents twenty-six true, first-hand accounts of spooks, spirits, and hauntings across the state of California, each published here for the first time. The book introduces many cases involving normal people who suddenly find themselves in bizarre paranormal situations. Told in the witnesses' own words, each case is illustrated by award-winning artist Christine Kesara Dennett. Learn what happens when homes are built over a Native American Burial Ground. Read how it feels to be hugged by a friendly ghost. Find out what to do when a ghost tries to choke and possess you. Join four young teen-aged boys who use themselves as bait to attract a hostile ghost called the White Witch. Also, visit a woman who received conclusive physical proof of life after death from the spirit of her deceased ex-husband, and find out how Charles Manson's notorious crimes left a trail of severely haunted houses. These are only a few of the amazing true accounts presented in this ghostly collection, and a full range of ghostly phenomena are presented, some funny, some scary, and some absolutely bone-chilling. All of them are true. Whatever you do, don't read this after dark!

Size: 6" x 9"   26 illustrations   192 pp.
ISBN: 0-7643-1972-8   soft cover $14.95

The Ghosts of New Orleans. Dr. Larry Dr. Larry Montz, and Daena Smoller. New Orleans is haunted. Its rich culture and stormy history make the city a haven for supernatural activity. Based on a six-year scientific study by the International Society for Paranormal Research (ISPR), this book separates facts from folklore and local legends, taking the reader on a fascinating trip through more than 25 different haunted properties. Spend a night in the Bourbon-Orleans Hotel, where there are many guests besides the ones on the registry. Stop by O'Flaherty's Irish Channel Pub, and find out why there are security bars on the third floor windows. Step aboard light aircraft carrier USS Cabot to encounter crew members who were lost years ago in a kamikaze attack. In addition to the thrill and suspense of the profiles themselves, this book is a firsthand account of paranormal research. ISPR, founded in 1972, is an internationally renowned organization devoted to the study of ghosts and the paranormal. The group has investigated properties worldwide, often with amazing results. With these expert guides, prepare for a fabulous tour of a spectacular city!

Size: 6" x 9"	48 illustrations	160 pp.
ISBN: 0-7643-1184-0	soft cover	$14.95

Savannah Spectres. Margaret Wayt Debolt. Savannah and the Georgia coast, with its old plantations, huge ancient oaks hung with Spanish moss, and tales of pirates, wars, fevers, African voodoo, and other supernatural doings, has always been a legendary and tragically romantic place. In this book, antebellum estates, house museums, long-conquered forts, and restored townhouses are visited with a noted psychic investigator in order to learn what it is like to live and work in these places today. The result is some seventy stories, skillfully interwoven with the heritage of the area's colorful past, and illustrated with over thirty photos and sketches by local artists. Incidents of precognition, extrasensory perception, deja vu and possible reincarnation are included in this personal and highly readable account of a search for the deeper meaning of life and death through psychic experience.

Size: 5 1/2" x 8 1/2"	30+ photos/illustrations	200 pp.
ISBN: 0-89865-201-4	soft cover	$9.95

Baltimore's Harbor Haunts: True Ghost Stories. Melissa Rowell & Amy Lynwander. Baltimore, Maryland, has harbor neighborhoods that have a long and colorful history of industry, immigrants, and ghosts. This spellbinding book exposes some of their unknown scary histories and uncovers 37 hauntings along the water. From the ghost of a drowned boy in Canton to the famous haunts of Fort McHenry, tantalizing stories pay homage to the people who remained behind. Meet the more "spirited" residents of the Canton, Fell's Point, Inner Harbor, Federal Hill and Locust Point neighborhoods, including the ghost with a favorite polka on the juke box and the lady who rewards cleanliness with money. Featuring 68 b/w photos of the haunted sites, this spooky volume is not to be missed.

Size: 6" x 9"	68 b/w photos	160 pp.
ISBN: 0-7643-2304-0	soft cover	$14.95